I0764639

THE ZIGZAG XANADU

Novels by Dennis Bowen

International Thriller Series

THE WATER DIAMONDS
Book 1

THE BLACKSTONE PERFECTION
Book 2

THE CRYSTAL SEDUCTION
Book 3

THE REDROCK QUARANTINE
Book 4

THE FINAL MASQUERADE
Book 5

THE VIRTUE TRANSITION
Book 6

THE JASMINE NEGATIVE
Book 7

THE GOSPEL LABYRINTH
Book 8

THE KINDRED HERITAGE
Book 9

The Backstory Files

STONES

THE ZIGZAG XANADU

Dennis Bowen

The Zigzag Xanadu is a work of fiction. Names, characters, places, and incidents are the products of the author's imagination or are used fictitiously. Any resemblance to actual events, locales, or persons, living or dead, is entirely coincidental.

Copyright © 2025 by Dennis Bowen
All rights reserved
ISBN: 979-8-9997632-0-4
www.facebook.com/DennisBowenThrillers
www.twitter.com/DBowenThrillers
www.DennisBowen.com
Book Interior Design by 52 Novels

ACKNOWLEDGMENTS

At the risk of repeating myself, thank you to the readers worldwide who have immersed themselves in my *International Thriller Series*. While I create the intrigues that span the globe and enjoy every minute of it, in the end, I write these novels for you and your enjoyment. It's really that simple.

As with *The Water Diamonds, The Blackstone Perfection*, *The Crystal Seduction*, *The Redrock Quarantine, The Final Masquerade, The Virtue Transition, The Jasmine Negative*, *The Gospel Labyrinth*, and *The Kindred Heritage*, my appreciation and gratitude goes out to those who offered suggestions and encouragement during the writing of *The Zigzag Xanadu*.

I express appreciation to my fabulous editor, Laura Taylor. She has provided the editing prowess to insure a quality presentation for this series and for STONES, the initial offering of *The Backstory Files*.

As in life, each successive endeavor—such as writing a series of novels—is built on what came before. Any errors or omissions in *The Zigzag Xanadu* I claim as my own.

I extend my gratitude to family members and friends for their support, and to former colleagues, some of whom offered up their lives in the service of this great country, and whose presence in my life gives my International Thriller Series its noted sense of reality. Thank you to all.

Dennis Bowen

CHAPTER 1

There was nothing left to do … but die.

The product of what had just gone before.

• • •

It began at daybreak. Magus Crayle was up with the sun, and viewed a cloudless sky plus a nice breeze. He'd headed to the docks and boarded his 39-foot sailboat. A little motoring out of the ocean harbor, and he set the sails, caught the wind, and took his place at the helm.

Just a couple of restful hours out to sea, it happened.

A huge explosion nearly disintegrated the vessel.

Minutes later, he found himself floating on the only remaining piece large enough to support his size and weight.

• • •

The man reached high with his left hand.

He grasped the top of the mast in a vice grip.

With his right hand, he clasped the right-side tail of his heavy blue denim over-shirt.

He pulled it wide, catching as much of the substantial breeze as possible.

The tiny raft of flotsam picked up speed.

It had to.

There wasn't a moment to lose.

• • •

Three hundred yards astern, a submarine sail poked up, penetrating the icy-cold water's surface.

Admiral Lothar Schmidt ordered the periscope raised and peered into the aperture.

He focused on the man.

"Ready torpedoes," he ordered in his native German.

A psychiatric research doctor in a white lab coat, with a berm of matching hair, watched it all unfold on his 58" super high-definition monitor.

The CIA's latest technology.

CHAPTER 2

American president Kimbel Stones poked his special Smartphone with attitude. His ultra-resolution screen propped against the wall of the Oval Office went black. That he'd utilized his middle finger spoke volumes.

He glanced over at the doctor.

"Doc, your mind-messing psychiatric research for the Company—pardon, the CIA—is ruining some of the best minds we have. You're becoming a national security threat."

Doctor Pirmin Rorschach, under pressure, always devolved into Swiss-accented English.

"I haff proceeded with mine research strictly within scientific boundaries. Subject Crayle may haff intermittent memory loss, and a few serious heart beats, but he will recover in short time, as before."

"Doctor, he's still operational. Something could pop up at any time. Something we don't control. Like a crisis?"

Rorschach skipped over the rhetorical. "Mine best advice is to remind him of major facts—see how he reacts. That should get his mind back. If not, I haff a Plan B."

The doctor's smile wasn't returned. He went on.

"My Plan B? He needs to relax. Perhaps at his cabin at Big Bear Lake. In the mountains. You know, we haff mountains in Switzerland which produce a calming effect. Hmmm?"

President Stones had never killed a doctor of psychiatry. Right now, he wondered how good it would feel. He turned to Susanna. She looked her usual calm, rational thinking self. With her long ago service in the Israeli intelligence service, Mossad—not to mention her stint with its assassination element, Kidon—she could be relied upon as his most trusted confidant and supplier of sage advice. Even her hair, swept down and forward to points on each side of her face, added to her rock-solid stature.

"We need to let him recover a bit. Then, we'll try doc's Plan B. Go from there. With Luisa here helping, we'll get him back to operational."

She'd referred to Stones' press secretary. He'd worked with both ladies long ago at the San Ernestino Observer out on the Southern California coast just north of San Diego. From a small-town newspaper to the presidency. What a difference a day makes.

"Let's check in on him," Stones said as he stood and walked to the presidential bedroom.

There, in probably the most comfortable bed on the planet, lay Magus Crayle. Master spy. Drenched in sweat.

Luisa touched the back of her hand to his forehead.

"Little warm. Not bad for what he's been through."

All eyes panned to Rorschach, who simply shrugged his shoulders.

"I'd give him a kiss," Luisa said in her Brazil-sexual intonation, "but it wouldn't be right."

"No," said the woman the Secret Service agents had just brought into the room.

Hekka Crayle walked to her husband's bedside, leaned over, and planted one.

His eyes popped open.

His arms flew up. He pulled her to him.

As his hands started to move where they shouldn't in a public setting, he noticed the others.

"Oh!"

He fell back.

"Well," Susanna observed. "He remembers some things."

CHAPTER 3

Everyone stood silent as Crayle stared up at the ceiling.

Until President Stones special Smartphone emitted its ring tone, the opening guitar intro to the James Bond series theme songs.

"CIA," he announced to those present as he pressed PLAY.

"Yes."

He listened.

"Yes. And Jack, give Anastasia whatever she needs."

He listened.

"Yes … anything."

He pressed STOP.

Before anyone else could react, Crayle suddenly propped himself up on his right elbow.

"Anastasia Romanova. Czarina and effectively empress and sovereign of all Russia."

Out of character, Doc Rorschach applauded.

"Ferry goot, Herr Crayle."

He turned to the rest.

"Very good, I mean."

His exit from Swiss-accented English signaled he now felt less at risk. He turned back to his subject.

"More, Herr Crayle."

The doctor's research subject—or victim—stared off, not at all focused on the room's other inhabitants.

"She is the descendant of Czar Nicholas deposed by the Communist revolution. In 1917, as I recall. She hooked up with the Russian Federation President. To realize his ultra-authoritarian goals, he remanufactured himself as Czar Vladimir, affecting a permanent hold on the top political spot.

"After his assisted passing in South America, she became the leader, unencumbered by anything resembling democracy.

"She orchestrated an assemblage of his supporters at his casket at the Moscow Kremlin, then arranged for one of those Made-In-China mini-nukes to go off, taking them all—and a significant segment of Moscow—off the map. As in, forever. The absence of radiation gave away the China connection since they are the only ones who coat their nuclear bombs with a radiation sponge.

"She remains very friendly to us."

He left out the fact that she was, by reputation, noticeably voluptuous and sexual.

"She has that descendant of the Mad Monk, Rasputin, on hand as her trusted advisor, gofer, and consort."

Silence from the enraptured group.

Then, Rorschach joined in. "There. My subject is quite fine. We can proceed with my experiments."

President Stones threw a firm shake of his head to that notion.

"Over your own dead body, Doc. Suspend your experiments forthwith and, as a warning, I heard about a bunch of Italian singers who didn't obey those in charge. They later became known as the *castrati*."

He waited.

"*Capisce*?"

The doctor produced a puzzled look.

"Understand?"

Rorschach nodded.

"Yes, Godfather," drew a laugh from the others. The times were tense. Laughter provided some much-needed respite.

Crayle extended it.

"I don't remember the doctor having a sense of humor."

More laughs. And nodding heads.

He gave it a finishing touch.

"While I remember the leader of today's Russia and her near-term past, which is good, I need some rest, peace, and quiet."

"Alright," said Stones. "Everyone out. We'll do some lunch. See where we go from here. One memory down, but we'll need to take this a lot further. So much has transpired in just the past few years. He needs to remember it all. For our good. For the good of the country. Hell, for the good of the world."

They left.

Susanna closed the door.

Crayle dropped off.

• • •

Outside the president's bedroom, the five of them sat down to a table brought into the Oval Office for a casual bite to eat.

They all scooped up their selections from the Teddy Roosevelt buffet furniture, and took seats in no particular order.

Silence reigned until Hekka shared her observations.

"He's been through a lot leading up to now, and this psychiatric experimentation, as valuable to us as it could be, took him to the edge. He needs serious rest. Then, he's off to full-time Director of Central Intelligence, and into the public spotlight."

"You're right, Hekka," Susanna concurred. "We can poke his mind later. As far as the spotlight is concerned, we'll all need to pitch in to help him get accustomed. As you know, a spy's first need is to not be noticed. Then, if noticed, it's not to be remembered. Those are my former employer, Mossad's, two basic rules."

Stones, a former NSA operative, shook his head. "No. I believe those rules originated with *our* intel entities. We're good at sharing."

"Sharing with the Five Eyes? The intel agencies of the English-speaking allies?"

"FEPI. Five Eyes Plus Israel."

Smiles all around.

"Let's polish this off, and revisit our master spy. I'm having the future start now, not when he is fully recovered."

The group polished off the gourmet quality buffet, then trooped back into the bedroom.

"Rise and shine," the President bellowed in Crayle's direction.

"Rise and shine!"

CHAPTER 4

Crayle's eyes popped open, and he sat up with a gasp.

He couldn't have reacted more dramatically if they'd yelled out, "Happy Birthday!"

"Peace and quiet works here," he said. "Kimbel? Peace and quiet?"

"When we've bestowed peace and quiet to the rest of the world, then we can rest up. So here's what's next for your memory prompting. A name. Jean-Marc Lalumière. What say you, Mag?"

Crayle pondered. He had little choice. Give them what they want, and they'll go away, he thought.

"Son of Sylvain Lalumière. He was the descendant of French aristocrats. Most of them killed in the Reign of Terror after the revolution. Some of those Made-In-China nukes enabled him to reinstitute the French monarchy. He received the official crowning, and our old friend Patti Norbrunn ended his dream the same day. Then, Hekka ended Patti Norbrunn.

"Sylvain's son, Jean-Marc, succeeded him. He then hooked up with the Swedish queen. Who would've thought? A France-Sweden alliance concocted—no pun intended—and consummated in some bedroom."

"A royal bedroom."

"There's only one way to yell out *Oh, God!*" Lenny chimed in as he waltzed through the bedroom door.

Crayle glanced at a control panel on the wall next to him. "Is there a button here for *PRIVACY*?"

"Presidents don't have privacy," Stones observed.

Lenny helped out. "Yeah. The president could be screwin' the pooch."

The president turned. "There is no pooch screwing going on in my bedroom. That sort of thing is relegated to the Situation Room."

That one got a laugh.

"Then there's China," Crayle said, trying to move things along.

Susanna was intrigued. She'd heard the rumors of their master spy's sojourn in that country. "What do you remember?"

"I was sent over to mastermind a coup. As in the France experience, I was to provide one Chin Yao-wu with a strategy for taking down the Communist government, and re-institute the China empire of long ago. Notice that there's a trend established here. Similar to Sylvain, Chin had the creds of being a descendant of China's first emperor, Chin Xihuangdi, centuries before."

"With that we need to pause," said Lenny. "I need to go potty. I don't want to miss anything."

He walked to the presidential bathroom. As he stepped through the doorway, a bolt of electricity shot out from the jamb, knocking him to the floor.

"Facial recognition, Lenny. You're not me. It's part of that new artificial intelligence package the Secret Service is trying out. And … it works."

Stones leaned over the bed and pushed a button labeled BYPASS.

"There. If it's not too late, you can go in now. And I'm afraid I have stuff to do. This session is over. Mag remembers just fine. But, Doc, your research needs to be put ON HOLD with wherever that button is. Mag and crew need to get across the country to Big Bear Lake, and take a quick breather before the next phase begins. With Mag as the CIA's seventh floor. I'll be heading out soon to Las Vegas. Love to have y'all meet me there. Everyone in on the plan?"

Nods everywhere.

Almost.

Stones glare stopped Lenny short. He stood, and gingerly entered the presidential loo.

Inside, he checked the urinal for any superficial wiring.

• • •

The next day, Crayle, Hekka, Lenny, and Rorschach would be headed home. To their log cabins high in Southern California's San Bernardino Mountains. To Big Bear Lake.

Marli and Flori, who usually piloted the team's two Dassault Falcon business jets, did the honors.

From the small airport in the valley just North of Big Bear, the transport vehicle, an ambulance, belonged to the covert CIA hospital 300 feet below a gravel yard complex just West of the airport. It would deposit the doctor at his research hospital residence after it entered the special garage, and descended—by vehicle elevator—the 300 feet.

The Crayle team would, as they had many times before, be driven up the winding and narrow Highway 18.

They'd drop Lenny off at his place in Boulder Bay and the Crayles at their lakeside cabin in the tiny village, Fawnskin.

CHAPTER 5

Before Lenny could cause any serious animus toward the team, Crayle herded them off to Reagan International Airport just outside the nation's capitol.

They arrived at the section reserved for secret stuff. Nothing like telling the rest of the intel world that they'd best keep an eye on you. Relying on professional courtesy didn't always pan out in the Crayle team's sphere of reality.

Marli and Flori had the old Dassault Falcon 8X ready to fly. It was as if they possessed a crystal ball—or had received a heads-up call from the President to be ready.

That was good. They were loaded and in the air in fifteen, as Marli would say.

The consummate professional in handling presidential behests, she kept secret the fact that the man in the Oval Office asking for her services was her ex.

Four hours and change later, they landed at what they laughingly referred to as Kimbel Stones International, its single runway just long enough to handle the Falcon.

As usual, the team was off and into a waiting ambulance, courtesy of a nearby gravel yard. It served to mask and guard the covert hospital deep below.

There came a collective sigh of relief as they climbed the narrow and winding Highway 18 at pace.

Over to Big Bear City in a few and then to Lenny's place on the strikingly beautiful Boulder Bay.

Lenny's wife, Alona, stood outside to greet him.

"Come inside, you major league twerp. We need to talk."

He followed her inside, not knowing if she missed her intimacy with him during his absence, or if he was in trouble. Again.

Next, the ambulance curved around the Southwest side of the lake to stop at the MacKay residence. The log cabin's front yard no longer sported the Abrams tank that had caused some concern among neighbors, and appeared to the world like a normal mountain resort homestead. There was no indication regarding the secret gadgets the former Navy SEAL developed for the CIA's Science and Technology Department. Or of the comms his wife, Phoebe, received from her old boss at the FBI federal witness protection unit, asking her how soon she would be 'off loan' to the CIA's Other Specialized Staffs entity and back doing real work.

Last, the EMT vehicle rounded the Northwest corner of Big Bear Lake, proceeded through the little burg called Fawnskin, and turned onto the driveway connected to the Crayle's cabin.

In less than two minutes, the driver headed East and back down the 18.

Mission accomplished.

Until next time.

For Mag and Hekka Crayle, it was great to be back home.

Suitcases inside, they plopped onto the couch and breathed a second sigh of relief.

• • •

Back over in Boulder Bay, Lenny felt re-energized from the harrowing trip up Highway 18.

"Time for a recap … of me."

The applause was muted, if any.

Undaunted, Lenny recalled his early days. As early as grade school, he became known for his unique brand of humor. But not in a good way. He developed a knack for coming up with jokes, and then particularly enjoyed explaining them when no one laughed. Clearly, he was the intelligent one in the room. The others just didn't *get it.*

His father, Sammy, often advised young Lenny to get his intellect to show up in his grades. "Or I'll have to start a business so I can hire you—if no one else will."

This far along in life, he smiled that he remembered such Sammy-isms verbatim.

He missed his dad just as he missed his brother, Wolfram. The espionage business had not been kind. Both of them, murdered. Assassinated.

Alona entered the room and immediately noticed her husband deep in thought.

"Better watch that thinking thing. Might hurt your brain … again."

He rolled his eyes. Again. Sounding just like him. Lenny's humor was definitely a contagion.

"Almost time for lunch. We're headed over to barbeque with the Crayles and MacKays. Take a shower. I don't want their surveillance cams capturing me letting you out of the trunk. It wouldn't look good."

"You grew up some in West Hollywood."

"I grew up a lot in West Hollywood."

"What was that place that Micmac got his Les Paul guitar? Custom, as he calls it."

"West L.A. Music. Where all the Hollywood musicians got their gear."

"His birthday's coming up."

"I know someone who purchased a guitar like his in 1976. Maple top and fretboard. Mahogany back. Today, they wouldn't talk to you for less than three thousand dollars."

"Maybe I'll just go there and take a picture of one. He'd appreciate the effort."

"He couldn't play an effort. We'll get him a gift card. Guitar Center or Musician's Friend."

"Yeah."

She stared.

He jumped up from the sofa. "Shower!"

"I'll get little Lenny ready."

• • •

It wasn't a long drive to the Crayle's place. Perhaps a mile. They headed West, crossing the Big Bear Dam, then arced around the West end of Big Bear Lake, passing the MacKay cabin on their left.

"I liked the look better when Micmac had the Abrams tank in the front yard."

"Neighbors complained. Said it violated C, C, and Rs. Y'know. Covenants, Codes, and Restrictions."

Lenny knew that no one knowing the former SEAL with his 'serious as a heart attack' FBI wife would issue any sort of complaint.

Alona interrupted his train of thought.

"Looks like our son has fallen asleep. Oh … I forgot. Got a call from our travel agent."

"Got any new deals on cruises?"

"Not the real travel agent. Darryl. Who sets up our off-the-books spy trips."

"We're not going anywhere. I think we're done spying."

"No. He's never done this before. He's asking a favor."

"What? He wants me to do a standup comedy in his home town? Sydney, Nova Scotia?"

"He has someone he wants you to do your private investigator thing with. He needs someone from outside Canada. It's serious. Or he wouldn't ask."

"He can get someone else. I like it right here in Big Bear. And I doubt Nova Scotia has Serrano Burgers like the ones we're about to enjoy at Hekka's place."

"$100,000 a week, plus expenses."

"Uh … done!"

• • •

Alona steered them through the little village called Fawnskin as they swung around the Northwest corner of the lake.

Shortly, they pulled into the Crayles' driveway.

CHAPTER 6

Just after dawn, the rain began to fall on Big Bear Valley. Since rain doesn't even slow down a former Navy SEAL, Micmac rang the bell at the Crayle cabin front door.

Crayle lifted up off the couch, moaned, padded to the door, and let in his friend and cohort.

Micmac held up his latest device from the CIA's Science and Technology Directorate.

"Yeah, Mag, it's yet another gadget for the S & T boys and girls. The ultimate truth detector. 100% is the target. It'll change the world."

"So, instead of detecting deception, it detects the truth."

"Yeah." He reached over to a pair of clamps, each with a wire attached. "I'm guessing, but I'm thinking that testicles react a certain way when you tell the truth. Drop your drawers, and I'll connect you up."

"Have you been drinking water from that polluted stream? You're not getting anywhere near me with those clamps. And, unless women always tell the truth, your testicular approach only gets you half way there."

Just then, Phoebe burst in as if performing some violent entry effort for the FBI. Placing three bags full of groceries on the counter, she let out a gasp of relief.

"I like my husband's ballsy approach to problem solving." She glanced at one, then the other. "Get it?"

Crayle shook his head. "It's good we're into spying and police work around here. Our shot at standup comedy isn't something I'd bet on."

"Yeah," said the former SEAL. "I was kidding about the testicle thing. But not about a fool proof truth detector. Think about it. All you need is my setup in a courtroom. Defendant answers with the truth, he's done. Guilt and innocence is determined in a second or so. Refuse to answer … guilty."

"Guilty until proven innocent," Phoebe assessed. "I like that."

"There's a fly in your ointment, Micmac."

"I hate when that happens. Always having to buy new ointment."

"It has nothing to do with ointment. It has everything to do with the Fifth Amendment of the U.S. Constitution."

"Well, it's been amended a bunch of times," Phoebe advised. "One more won't hurt."

"When people tell the truth, they access the analytical side of their brains. When they make stuff up, it's the creative side. I think that's where you should go with this."

Micmac set aside his things. "Change of subject. What about that Pattie? Are we sure she and all her incarnations are done with?"

"Hekka took her out decisively at Versailles. Broke her heart. Literally."

"Just her and Nattie, who went out with a bang."

"Yeah, that little nuclear device she had did the deed. Death and cremation in the same millisecond."

"That's how you see if the forgiveness thing works. Pattie did prance around as Sister Magdalena. Might have saved some souls, don't you think?"

"I think her murdering the Mother Superior there in Spain might have etch-a-sketched any and all salvation prospects."

"Well, I need to get ready for a little trip," said Micmac. "By the way, have you ID'd yourself as the new DCI yet?"

"No. I go into Langley in disguise. Jack watches my back, and Kimbel has the only security clearance high enough to know everything."

"Way above Top Secret."

"The President's one hell of a good guy, but he can declassify anything in an instant, so keep watchin' your six."

"Will do, Micmac." Crayle peered over his shoulder. "Six in sight."

Phoebe, just finished recouping from her conquest of the groceries, tapped her phone. "Okay, José. We're outta here."

• • •

The Springtime sun was up the next day.

Hekka padded into the kitchen in her moccasins, and not much else.

Ten minutes later her husband arrived, waving the CIA Science and Technology Department's take on a handheld, secure communication device

"Just got off the phone with the President," Crayle said as he waltzed out of the Sound and Technology Isolated Bedroom, the STIB.

"You do this every time. How many times has he told you, practically ordered you, to call him by his first name?"

"Hmmm. Just got off the phone with Kimbel."

He gleamed as he took a seat at the dining table.

"So what did the unscrambled version of what he said … say?"

"You know we originally got Phoebe on loan from the FBI. She performed protection detail for high level Federal witnesses."

"Like the rock star."

"Yeah. Gleese, I think was his name. The guy got doped up after a concert and had his way with her."

"Then, on one of our many operational sojourns, she met up with him again."

"Yes. On the Queen Mary 2, headed for New York Harbor."

"You left out that the QM2 had aboard a mini-nuclear device intended to take out New York City."

"Minor omission."

"It was major, and was our mission."

"Why am I getting that 'wait for it' vibe?"

"That was when Phoebe Glocked the crap out of him."

He laughed hard.

Begrudgingly, his wife followed suit. Then, together, "Lenny humor is contagious."

"I heard that!"

Both heads snapped around.

In pranced the referenced private investigator.

He nearly collided with Crayle, who headed out to fetch some onions for the impending next round of Hekka's Serrano burgers.

CHAPTER 7

So, Phoebe had forgotten to bring onions. Serrano burgers without them were unforgivably incomplete.

Crayle motored out of Fawnskin, heading around the West end of Big Bear Lake, and across the dam. His Ford Cobra was conspicuous both in sight and sound, and decried any notion that an ultra-secret spy was at the wheel.

Arriving in Big Bear proper, he parked outside his favorite grocery store. He noted the passenger seat would hold a bag of onions, and not much else. Perhaps the six-point racing harness was a bit of overkill, but would keep the requisite vegetables safely secure.

Just then, a man approached. He appeared to be Germanic, and Crayle pushed back in his seat, feeling the cold steel of his pistol at his lower back.

The man, clad in lederhosen, smiled and raised his hand. What appeared to be a flat resemblance of a Bavarian pretzel dangled.

"Air freshener. Collecting donations for the Oktoberfest. Next October?"

Crayle shook his head, and accessed his wallet. His line of business had him ever on alert. Relax, he thought. He placed the pretzel on his mirror.

"*Vielen dank*," said the man, who saluted and walked away.

As he started to exit the Cobra, Crayle suddenly felt a bit weak. Then, he passed out.

When he awoke, he was bound to a chair. He heard the sounds of the *Rote Kreuz*, German Red Cross, jet as it coursed through the air. Standing directly in front of him, the man from the grocery store parking lot.

"We land shortly," was all he said.

"Mr. Crayle, it seems you have a relationship with the U.S. government. How do I know? You see, we Germans have always been adept at technology. We appreciate that which is precise. We left the mushy aspects of life to the French. To their credit, they mastered mushy to a level we could not have imagined."

"Your forbears weren't too happy with the French and their Grande Armée when they began their Franco-Prussian War in 1870."

"Precisely. We let down our resources as Germans and paid the price. We've done that again. In the past, we never allowed non-Germanic peoples to dilute the Master Race, as Herr Hitler characterized it. We are marching back. We shall soon lead my country, and Austria is set to join. We have some political debts to collect, but France, with its reinstituted monarchy, is not currently on the list."

"And the Russians?"

"Yes. The Russians. After the Second World War, they came into our country like the Slavs they are. They slaughtered men and boys, then turned their world-class sadism on the women … and girls. But their recent evolution to Czarina Anastasia …"

"She and her ancestors had nothing to do with the brutal Communist regimes of Lenin, Stalin, and the rest. With focus on elevating Russia using proven economics, the people are quite capable of educated risk-taking and hard work. The resulting boom will allay any notions of geopolitical aggressions."

"You learned this strategy from the Czarina? In Saint Petersburg? Between gasps?"

"How, where, and when I learned it is my little secret. But it is real."

"Perhaps the new world order shall be one of peaceful coexistence, not military aggression. I envision leadership from America, China, Russia, and, of course, Germany."

Crayle didn't wish to call out the ego-thumping Karl engaged in. Perhaps another time.

And Magus Crayle had a potential ace up his sleeve. He was now 'road testing' a new CIA Science & Technology device for Micmac. Its name: Truth Teller. Doctor Rorschach embedded it in a new cochlear implant. "Better than a cock implant," he'd joked.

Crayle asked: "If it's perfected according to the doctor, then why isn't it operational?"

The answer: "It would prevent superiors from lying to subordinates ... especially operatives. The necessary lies. You know."

CHAPTER 8

Hours after leaving Big Bear Valley, the fake Red Cross jet landed in Switzerland. A black Mercedes SUV drove up to the parked plane, and the two men inside came aboard. They placed Crayle on a stretcher and secured him with his arms and legs still bound. They waved a bottle of the same scent that impregnated the air freshener and covered the unconscious spy with a blanket.

A half hour later, they arrived at a stereotypical Swiss chalet. They transported their captive inside, and revived him.

Crayle woke sitting in a relic wooden chair, and felt that someone from his past was staring at him.

Aryan Alliance chief Otto had a relationship with Iranian Aryans. Common ground? They hated the Jews. Just as did Adolph Hitler.

The mountains nearby were high and angular. They'd been that way for many thousands of years. As the sun bid adieu to the West, the temperature, even at Winter's end, dropped quickly.

"You are familiar with the mountains, Mister … I don't know what to call you."

"Kidnappers generally have a singular focus, I've heard. Perhaps you're the type who kidnaps novelists."

The driver laughed. "One who writes spy novels."

Crayle nodded. "That explains my travels. My writing style inculcates the flavors of the world as I've experienced them. And my name is well known. It's on all my book covers."

"Ah, yes. Magus Crayle. A pen name, no doubt. What is your birth name, then?"

"It's as on the books. I don't use a pseudonym. No need."

"Yes. You would only have that need if you were a spy. *Ja*?"

"Now there's an idea. Stories about a spy that was a writer of international espionage as a cover. Why didn't I think of that?"

"Then how do you explain having all those spy notions necessary for your stories?"

"Hmmm. I should call them spydeas. Spy plus ideas. My editor just loves when I make up new words."

"But how do you know those things?"

"Intuitively obvious, *Mein Herr*."

"I love it when you use the fancy English terms. It's so … Germanic."

"Love?"

"Ha. I am not, as you say, a gay man. Love has many levels. And you are not safely restrained in your seat motivated by my feelings."

"Which begs the question …"

CHAPTER 9

With Mag Crayle back from Switzerland, the president had definitely swung into campaign mode. And since elections characteristically were a crapshoot, he'd chosen Las Vegas as his jump start venue. Actually, Susanna and Luisa had chosen it.

Kimbel Stones had set some records, one in particular of him being the very first Libertarian to own the Oval Office. He was protective of that, but politics being what it was, he was overheard saying what really needed protection was his oval orifice. The comment drew laughs from all present except himself.

The town known colloquially as Sin City had recovered fully from a previous rather violent visit by the Crayle team. Festivity now ruled each day.

He sat in the presidential suite with a rather homeless-looking individual who'd introduced himself as Willie Maykit. Once Susanna had shown the pre-approved scruff into the room and departed, Stones stepped over to him and extended his hand.

"Mag, it's great to see you."

"I wondered out loud if I'd make it one more time. Maybe supply an election-winning strategy. I've got that, by the way, in here." He patted the scruff trench coat inside chest pocket. "Can't lose."

"If your past strategic successes are any indication, you're right. I do hope no miniaturized nuclear devices are required. As you know, with our Middle East successes, we're on the way to a ubiquitous peace. Susanna gave me that word—ubiquitous. Told me to find a place to use it."

"More likely, she told you to find a place to stick it."

Stones grinned. His assistant, Susanna, was still strong, but softened since her long ago experiences in the Israeli Mossad's assassination unit.

"A bit of business. I know you want to get home after your unexpected visit to Switzerland. You need to be more careful when you get involved with any sort of holiday planning. Especially Christmas."

"Yes. That much-needed R & R after the to-do in Washington had me dropping my guard. I'm lucky the Aryan Alliance wanted to offer a peace treaty. It took a face-to-face with their leader. The word from the top, so to speak."

"In Switzerland?"

"They've always seen it as one big safe house. Some guy named Adolph built the previous Aryan Alliance. Took over Germany in '33, I recall. This guy's different."

"His name?"

"Otto."

"Wasn't there one or more Ottos in the past? In our time?"

"Took 'em down. This Otto comes on like a conservative. Like some of our Republicans."

"Well, we'll keep tabs on their comms. Don't need to interrupt the peace we've got going."

"With that, I need to get back to Big Bear."

"When can you start running the Company full-time? You know. Seventh floor? Full time? Langley?"

Crayle waited through the rhetorical.

"I'm thinking soon, Mag. Jack's doing a good job—you're who I need long term."

Stones turned toward the door.

"Susanna!"

She stepped in.

"Please get this gentleman back home."

"Done and done, Mr. President."

Crayle stood and the two shared a brief hug.

Susanna had him back to the airport and aboard the Falcon in fifteen.

In his favorite of the jet's plush seats, he started to relax.

CHAPTER 10

Micmac arrived early to the Crayle's Big Bear cabin. He went behind to the lake side, propped up a ladder against the two seven-foot rosewood posts next to the redwood deck, shinnied up, and installed the latest spy gadget from the CIA's Science and Technology Directorate.

Phoebe had come along to help. She used her FBI Agent strength to ensure the ladder—and her husband—stayed in place. She twisted her head toward Hekka, who'd just stepped out onto the deck.

"These devices are directional. Sounds emanating from anywhere on your deck are countered with an equal and opposite sound that are pushed outward. Any surveillance attempts beyond the deck would be thwarted."

"Well, good morning, all. Welcome to the Mag and Hekka Crayle abode for what seems like a monthly barbeque. Save for any geo-political catastrophes that might intervene. With that, here's my hubby, also known as DCI Crayle, with a word. I'm shifting to the outdoor kitchen over there." She pointed at the barbeque.

Before she could move, Crayle produced and handed to her a brown, woven bag.

She peered inside.

"And here are my onions—for the Serrano burgers."

"Not just any onions," said her husband. "These are Swiss."

Lenny, who'd just arrived with his wife, Alona, couldn't let that go. "He probably picked them up … in Switzerland." He waited for the laugh that came.

"You're right, Lenny. Swiss onions that aren't fresh are not for my best friends."

Hekka set to cooking her signature burgers and slicing the truly fresh Swiss onions. Sliced tomatoes, pepper-jack cheese slices, and buns fresh form a local bakery rounded out the fare.

The redwood picnic table had been modified with the addition of two solid metal rails powered by an anti-magnetic repulsion system, courtesy of the CIA's S & T Department.

With Crayle, Micmac, Phoebe, Alona, and Lenny seated, Hekka placed a metal tray with burgers supported by the force field, and provided instructions.

"The table is quite old, and its top no longer smooth. Scooting a tray could cause problems. The tray, floating a couple inches above the table can be moved along in either direction. But be sure to just touch the top of the tray to move it, not underneath."

Lenny, not one to take instruction well, reached under.

He was rewarded with a shock that nearly pitched him onto the deck.

Worse, the tray, with its force field interrupted, nearly toppled and sent the delicious feast to its demise on the deck next to Lenny.

Fortunately, the calming fingertips of Crayle and Alona steadied the tray.

Lenny stood, dusted himself off, and rejoined the team.

They fairly assaulted the assortment and loaded up their plates.

Halfway through, Lenny was the first to speak.

"As I may have mentioned to some of you, we got a call from our travel agent, Darryl. Needs some P.I. help out there in Nova Scotia.

I'll be outta here for a while. So, Mag, consider that when you're passing out spy assignments with that new label of yours."

"Label? DCI? USA?"

"Yeah, that title."

"More than just a title," Hekka opined. "Why, I believe our explosives and gadget expert, Micmac, has already rigged some special business cards for Mag. They explode 24 hours after non-registered fingers touch them."

That drew a laugh from everyone.

Micmac began to consider the possibilities.

She continued. "I will need to complete my PhD research next. As soon as I get everything together, I'll be off to Eastern Russia for at least a couple of weeks."

While everyone clapped their approval, they didn't hear the cabin's front door open.

The Crayle's home security phone apps did.

A special chirp, and they both reached toward the small of their backs.

No need.

In walked a familiar face.

"Kimbel!"

Crayle reconsidered.

"Mr. President!"

Then, "Kimbel!"

The president shook his head with a smile.

"I was in the neighborhood, and thought I'd stop by."

"Stop by? You and Air Force One? And your Secret Service detail?"

"Mag, I've considered our conversation in Vegas. You need to relax big time. I'll set things up. You know. Take care of business."

Hekka reacted. "I'm the one who takes care of Mag's business."

"Just sayin' hi, Hekka. Gotta go. Business in D.C."

The president waved and, with his entourage in tow, left.

CHAPTER 11

"Well, the president gave me orders, Micmac. Go relax for a couple of weeks. No work. What do you think?"

"Easy. A cruise. We just won't tell him which one."

Crayle laughed at that one.

"Let's see. He has 17 or so intel agencies reporting to him in daily briefings. 'Sorry we can't find your new DCI, Mr. President.' He'd shoot them dead right then and there."

"Or delegate it. Look, a cruise is a great idea. I'll get our TA on the line."

"T & A? That had a vulgar connotation in the Navy."

"Travel Agent."

He entered the direct dial code. Nova Scotia Darryl answered his exceptionally Smartphone on the first ring.

"Hey, Magus. How the hell are you?"

"I'm fine. Say, Micmac is here with me. I have you on speaker. We need an R & R voyage—no guns, no bombs. Can you help us out?"

"Yes. Your president called. Said you'd be touching base with me."

The two men glanced at each other, and shook their heads.

"Someday, I'll actually have that thing we call privacy," Crayle observed.

"Retiring doesn't help. Not in this espionage business. You have to die for them to leave you alone."

"Alright. Privacy notion transferred to back burner. Can you get us something out of Fort Lauderdale … headed East?"

"Let me check."

They waited.

"There. Tomorrow. 1 P.M. Heads across to an island in the East Atlantic, then on to North Africa, and then the Med. You'll fly home. I'll arrange you two to Fort Lauderdale. Then, the flight back. It'll be pilot Marli or Flori. On the Company jet."

Crayle and Micmac got the reference to the CIA's off-the-books business jet of choice. One of the Dassault Falcons.

"Be at the airport in time for a 10 A.M. liftoff. About three hours in the air."

"For a four-and-a-half-hour transit by scheduled airline? Not bad."

"The limo will pick you up at the Crayle cabin … nine-ish."

"The limo that looks a lot like an ambulance?"

"That's the one."

"Thanks, Darryl."

They rang off.

• • •

The two men exited the STIB—the Sound & Technology Isolated Bedroom—and found the other four members of their team in the living room. They related the impending arrangements.

"That works," Lenny said. "I'll go do a little job for Darryl in Nova Scotia, and take my time with it. I'll charge by the hour."

"Darryl has a world-class sense of humor, but one that has boundaries."

"Thanks, Mag. To be fair, he probably won't get my jokes. He speaks Canadian, eh?"

Crayle turned to his wife, who had her own to-do list.

"That works. I need to perform a bunch of research in Asia. For my doctorate. I'll get Ling on the line. She'll arrange everything."

Phoebe chimed in. "Add me to the passenger manifest, Hekka. This works. Micmac'll have Mag's back. I'll have yours."

"What about me?" Lenny whined.

The four glanced over to Lenny's wife, Alona.

"I'm with client, gang. Lenny will go as a private investigator, not a spy. No one will notice. We're fine."

• • •

The next day, Crayle and Micmac, with roll-along suitcases, were delivered to the Falcon.

Marli as pilot, and Flori as co-pilot, greeted them. Then took them to Fort Lauderdale.

CHAPTER 12

The two vacationing spies rested on the flight, which landed at precisely three hours as Darryl had predicted. A short rideshare to the shipping port later, they checked in with their fake passports, then boarded the cruise ship.

"The Island Princess," Micmac observed. "Love the Sea Witch painted nice and big on the bow."

"Well, if the kind Sea Witch will watch over us, this should be an uneventful trip."

"Uneventful? We won't know how to behave."

They both chuckled.

• • •

They found their way to adjacent cabins replete with a connecting door. Their suitcases, checked in when they'd arrived, sat just inside.

Crayle found a note on the desk.

"Compliments of Mister K. Stones. Relaxing spa treatment scheduled for 5 P.M. Eastern Standard Time. Today."

Crayle checked his watch. "We arrived on board at 1 P.M. West Coast Time. That's 4 P.M. here. I'll unpack and head up. Boy, Kimbel is really serious about me relaxing. Starting day one."

"Skip the unpack, and head up now. Maybe they can take you early. I'll come along. We can head straight for some chow when they're done with you."

At the check-in desk, they each received a medallion and lanyard. It was a near-field device that unlocked the cabin door when the wearer was in close proximity. It had the added feature that would track them around the ship, wherever they went.

• • •

They arrived at the spa complex in fifteen minutes. Crayle observed that the woman in charge was quite intelligent, friendly, and would have been attractive to him had he not been indelibly married to Hekka—the American Indian woman with a 10-inch Bowie knife.

"Hi, Mister Crayle. Your medallion has checked you in. My name is Kelly."

She extended her hand, which he met with his own.

"And behind you is Tracy, who will be giving your massage. The physical relaxation will translate into mental relaxation."

"That's precisely what I need," Crayle responded.

"Mr. MacKay can take a seat here. Tracy will escort you to a private room."

Micmac took a seat, and Crayle followed Tracy down a passageway to Room 3.

"You'll have to undress, Mr. Crayle."

"Uh … everything?"

"There will be no premium massage, Mr. Crayle. And, yes. Everything. Then hop onto the bed and cover yourself with the sheet."

Before he could respond, she turned away.

He did as commanded, and was on the bed in short order.

She turned back to face him.

"On your stomach, please. I'll put on some aromatic essence to help you relax."

He did, and she did. His head faced the wall such that he couldn't see her.

"It's pine scent. Like you have in abundance in Big Bear."

Big Bear? How could she …

He went to turn his head, but it felt heavy. Still, he managed to turn it. He saw that she wore a gas mask. Just before he passed out.

The door opened. In stepped Micmac.

He turned to the masseuse.

"Nicely done, Tracy."

CHAPTER 13

Later, Crayle recovered from the relaxing massage and the even more relaxing induced sleep.

"So, Micmac, what's the itinerary for my relax away-from-work, away-from-home, away-from-all-stress vacation?"

"It's on your phone. Tap the Itinerary app."

Crayle drew the CIA Smartphone from his pocket, found the app, and tapped it.

The initial page appeared.

"Seven days at sea getting us from Fort Lauderdale to Madeira. The Portuguese island."

"Where—"

"No, no. Let's test my memory. Doctor Rorschach may be listening on my cochlear implant, so I need to get this right."

"What you need is a soundproof ear cover on that side."

"*I heard that* just came over the implant. With a Swiss accent."

They laughed.

Crayle held up a hand.

"I begin. We went to that island. Into the principal city of Funchal. Of significance, I convened Summit One. The Pope, Grand Ayatollah, and Chief Rabbi comprising the One God world leaders."

"You shamed them into supporting a world peace movement, as I recall."

"Same trip, you sat in with a rock band playing there."

Micmac nodded.

"The Apostles."

"Yes. The cover for four British MI-6 spies."

"It worked," Micmac observed.

"And I remember their names. Matthew, Mark, Luke, and Jane."

"Great cover. They did what they needed to do, by doing what they loved to do."

"You sat in, and performed Secret Agent Man."

"The crowd loved it."

"And no one knew."

"Except the spies."

"Us."

Two smiles and two mild head shakes.

"Mag, what's everyone going to do while we're gone?"

"Well, Lenny's got to finish gathering intel for Alona's current case. Then, he's off to help Darryl with whatever he has that requires outside-of-Canada help."

"And ..."

"Darryl, our esteemed covert travel agent, has history—good history—with the Royal Canadian Mounted Police. Their intel and covert ops side. It appears there's something going on they don't need to know about."

"Or they need *not* to know about."

"I hope he's not in any trouble."

"Mag, you are not to worry about his situation, or any other. This here former Navy SEAL, underwater explosives and weapons expert, Mick MacKay, is ordering you to relax."

Crayle breathed in, and slowly exhaled.

"Yes. Relax."

That voice came from Tracy, who'd appeared from nowhere, bearing a tray with two wedge-shaped glasses plus a separate, covered tray.

"Dry vodka martinis, shaken, not stirred."

The men took the glasses and quaffed them in one go.

"And now," Tracy added, "it's time for your wrap."

She drew a hot towel from under the tray cover, and gently wrapped it onto Crayle's face.

He had one last word.

"Well, here's to the end of what has been. A more than interesting working life. On to a boring desk job at Langley. When we set sail, it marked the end to all the violence and destruction that came before."

And it really was the end.

The end … of the beginning.

• • •

The next day came soon enough for Mag Crayle and Mick MacKay.

For the latter, it was back to work. Getting his colleague to relax. Getting him to talk. Testing his memory.

"You gave me Lenny and the look forward for him. How about Hekka?"

"Let's see. Hekka has, in her spare time, completed all classes for her PhD. She's taking her comprehensive tests as we speak, will undoubtedly pass, and her dissertation is all that's left. To finish up her research on the long ago migrations of her ancestors, she needs to visit Siberia."

"I don't believe you can just *visit* Siberia. There are probably books written on how to *survive* Siberia."

"True. But with her intel experiences on our team, her very developed natural survival skills, and talents …"

"Thanks in no small amounts to her Serrano Indian dad, and her Finnish mom."

"She should be leaving Big Bear about the time we reach Madeira. Off to Ling An-yee's little palatial abode in Hong Kong. Ling'll take care of everything. She and Phoebe will probably give Lenny a ride to the airport."

"I pray Lenny doesn't screw it up."

"I don't remember you ever praying, Micmac."

"I actually did. But only over the bodies of some really bad players. Sent them off to Eternal Hell, where they belonged."

"If I ever again see the three wise men—the world's top One God clerics—I'll pass on the high level of your devotion."

"You may want to skip that, Mag. I have enough 'splainin' to do come Judgment Day."

• • •

The Grand Ayatollah sat alone.

Sweat covered his hands. He'd wipe them on a holy towel, only to repeatedly succumb to the same drenching perspiration. The prospects of tomorrow's 'item' fell collectively on his shoulders alone. What, after all, could one person—a sole individual—accomplish?

Then, he remembered that perpetual fly in the ointment, Jesus Christ. While he consistently pushed aside the notion of Christ as the Son of God, Ayatollah Jahni could appreciate that level of backup horsepower for what he had ahead.

His basic strategy would allow the Parsi, Rustom Modi, to try to rule that which cannot be governed—a reconstructed Persia.

Beyond all of the surface noise, Jahni planned to put in place the reconstruction of the entire Middle East. As Muslim. With him at the top.

Looking back, a giant tidal wave from the Caspian Sea—caused by one of the Chinese miniature nuclear devices—had struck Tehran's government buildings. By the time rescuers arrived from neighboring towns, rescue had become recovery. The collection and identification of bodies.

All other ayatollahs and underlings perished. Along with the top echelons of the IRGC and Quds Force.

Grand Ayatollah Jahni was now alone. But, he reasoned, it was a good alone. No one left on the clerical side to challenge his ultimate authority or question his Islamist strategies and tactics.

The bad news: no one to carry them out, either. It turned out the Parsi, Rustom Modi, would give him some breathing room by assuming the temporary mantle of leader. Of Iran. Under the temporary misnomer, Persia.

Time to plot. And scheme.

CHAPTER 14

Darryl sat at his desk, an ornate wooden one with serious history. He peered out the window at the Bras D'Or body of water in the distance, just Southwest of Nova Scotia's Sydney Harbour. He pondered for the fiftieth time whether to call in resources from the Crayle spy team.

To the point, he'd provided 'travel agent' services to the team for their off-the-books CIA efforts many times.

He spotted a taxi headed his way. He hopped up, and stepped outside.

The taxicab screeched to a halt. A diminutive man swung open the door, and jumped out.

Crayle team member, Lenny Lipschitz.

The driver was also out of the cab. The two men argued as Darryl approached.

"You drive like a crazy Canadian," Lenny yelled. "The hell with giving you a tip! Now give me my luggage!"

Surprisingly, the driver said nothing. He just proffered his open and empty hand.

Darryl, ever the peacemaker, pulled a Canadian $50 bill from his pocket, and pasted it into the driver's hand.

In short order, Lenny wheeled his suitcase inside as the taxi driver squealed away.

"Well, how the hell are you, Mr. Lipschitz? Uh, Lenny?"

"Just great. That one must've checked the lunatic box when he applied for his license."

"Ah, yes. The lunatic box. It provides for additional insurance coverage."

Lenny caught the humor, and laughed.

"How about a beer, old friend? Molsons Canadian."

Lenny took a seat, accepted the ice cold bottle, and quaffed half in one take.

"This is good."

"We drink enough that we have a government beverage control agency to keep the supply chain going. You'll see people leaving the ABC stores with shopping carts full of booze. Drinking seems a national pastime."

"So the cold beer serves as a cool down in the warmer months, and the harder stuff as an alcohol-based, personal antifreeze during the winter."

"Just so."

"So, what is it you need, Darryl? I'm still a licensed P.I. in the States, and can find stuff. I understand you have the need for my services, but why not just use your associates at the RCMP?"

"One, I have no Mounties as associates. I'm an independent contractor. That way, I can work with any agency without having to engage in their turf wars."

"Yeah. It works that way in the U.S."

"Okay. We'll finish up on the Molsons, and we're out of here. I'll fill you in on the way."

"Way?"

"Yes. What I know, what I need you to find, and how I'll pay all your expenses and—oh, yeah—can't do this myself because I'm full up on keeping your team going here and there. Hekka, Phoebe, Mag, Micmac, Alona."

"Alona is stuck in Big Bear on a case. She's a defense attorney, but you know that. So, where to?"

"It's a lovely place called Baddeck. Not far. It's actually symbolic of people who try to discover things. Like P.I.'s do."

• • •

Ten minutes later they headed Southwest with their driver and guide, Diana.

Past the Northern portion of the gorgeous lake Darryl had mentioned, and soon into the parking lot for the Chanterelle Restaurant in the town, Baddeck.

They savored some delicious Nova Scotia lobster.

Then, off to the nearby Alexander Graham Bell Museum.

They checked out the many old phones propped on one wall, then Diana took a firm grip on Lenny's hand, and pulled him into the museum store.

There, he received a wrapped box approximately five inches by four inches by three inches high.

Lenny reached for his wallet, but Diana grasped his arm.

"Darryl's got this."

Off they went, retracing the route back to Sydney and Darryl's place.

Soon, Lenny was on his way South.

To Halifax.

By ship.

CHAPTER 15

Lenny arrived on the cruise ship, Emerald Princess, at Canadian Nova Scotia's capitol, Halifax. Quickly off the ship, he produced an excursion ticket to the nearest port agent to obtain the necessary colorful shirt sticker. It identified the tour and bus number, presumably so he, a licensed private investigator, would not get lost. A cute Indonesian woman peeled the sticker, and pasted it on his shirt.

"I'd rather you stick it on, like tonight at say 8 o'clock."

With her tan skin tone, it was a challenge to turn red, but she managed.

Lenny, seeing her embarrassment, saved the day with, "Hey, I was just kidding. I wouldn't cheat on Alona … with you."

The young woman's thoughts changed to considering justifiable homicide. "Edward," she pointed, "will direct you to the gangway."

Edward, not his actual Filipino name, did so.

Lenny walked through the exit procedure, pressing his wrist-worn electronic medallion to a small, waist-level screen. It verified the medallion by producing a file portrait on a separate small computer screen. It looked exactly like the P.I.

He passed through and ambled a distance down an enclosed walkway. He always knew when he was leaving a safe location for a far riskier one.

Like now.

On the dock he located the tour bus, which sported a front window card with his sticker color and number. He handed the tour guide his excursion ticket.

"Like my name badge says, Mr. Lipschitz, I'm Angela. I'll hook you up as requested. By Darryl."

"Define hook me up."

Angela just smiled, and motioned him toward the open bus door.

The guide was attractive enough, but those kinds of thoughts always took him back to his wife. To Alona. If he ever messed around, they'd never find his body. Maybe a piece or two.

• • •

Following an hour-long drive through Nova Scotia's beauteous scenery, they stopped at Mercator Vineyards for a little wine tasting.

Lenny easily played the part of the visiting tourist, acting and looking nothing at all like an American spy.

"I really like the restored farmhouse look for the tasting room. Hmmm?"

"It's actually a restored farmhouse, Mr. Lipschitz. We don't do 'phony' in Nova Scotia."

Finishing, she moved them on to L'Acadie Vineyards, and more tastings.

Lenny discovered that, when wine was free, there was a link between tasting and toasted. Beyond the alliteration.

Then off to their final stop. The Domaine de Grand Pré in the eponymous village.

Its Le Caveau Restaurant provided a fare substantive and tasty enough to dilute the quantities of wine imbibed prior.

Ready to leave, Angela got the check, and something else.

She motioned Lenny to a quiet corner.

"Here," she said as she handed him the package. "Put that into your backpack. Keep it with you. Always."

Minutes later, they were on their way back to Halifax.

And the next step in his journey.

Right after a quick stop back home.

CHAPTER 16

The time had come. And it arrived on a perfect day.

Hekka Crayle had her two suitcases packed, each about two-thirds full.

She left room for artifacts she'd pick up on her research tour of Siberia. If there was a trail of artifacts left by her ancestors during the Great Migration from Asia to North America, she intended to track them down. Having one of the top FBI Agents, Phoebe, along was a major plus.

Phoebe arrived by Uber with her own pair of suitcases. Then, Lenny showed up.

"Here," his driver and wife, Alona, said, "I'm formally placing him in your custody … uh, care. I expect him back in a couple of weeks." She glanced over at her husband. "Don't dally, Lenny, my sweet. I'll have a nice long list of honey-do's to get you back in the game."

"I'll be in the game the whole trip. Darryl's gonna owe me big time. And I won't see these two after the airport today. I believe Flori is taking me East to Sydney, Nova Scotia. Marli's taking them …" He waved at Hekka and Phoebe. "… to Hong Kong."

"Well, you say hi for me to that Brazil-sexual Flori, and keep your hands and your thoughts to yourself."

She handed him a photo. "Here. This is one of Little Lenny and me, to help you remember."

He took the proffered photo, and glanced at it.

"What's with the handgun on the desk there?"

"The purpose of the photo is to help you remember. That's all."

She smiled, then drove off.

"We're all here. Have luggage. Passports?"

Nods from Lenny and Phoebe.

Hekka pointed at the road.

"Here comes our ride."

The CIA's faux ambulance pulled into the driveway. The driver hopped out and loaded the luggage in the back. There was room for that, for the three travelers, and for the body in the bag. He saw their concern.

"Oh, he won't bother you. He's going with Mr. Lipschitz on the plane. Have to multi-task these days." He smiled.

The ambulance made the trip East across the Big Bear plateau, then a little more rapidly than those in back liked, down the winding two-lane Highway 18. While the others made noises of discomfort from time to time, the extra passenger remained docile.

The two Dassault Falcon business jets were ready to load when they arrived. Both Marli, with her bright red lipstick and substantial Hollywood sunglasses, and the sexy Brazilian, Flori, wore big smiles.

"Weather's lookin' great, y'all can have whatever fun you like … with those phone apps. Other than that, drinks are on the house, the President sends his best wishes, and let's go!"

It was as Marli had prophesied. Lenny's flight East was smooth. Instead of locking the flight deck door so she wouldn't have to hear him whine, Flori turned control over to her co-pilot, a former Navy fighter jet jockey. She stepped back into the cabin, and fed Lenny a very well aged bottle of Bordeaux, compliments of President Stones.

• • •

It was the same vintage on the flight West. Ten hours to Hong Kong. After a bottle of classic red wine each, Hekka and Phoebe stretched out on the full-sized bed in the aft part of the cabin. They were out before the third hour.

• • •

Hekka and Phoebe were awakened by a sudden change in speed. The intercom explained.

"Comin' into HKG, gang. Hong Kong International Airport. Also known as Chek Lap Kok International Airport. Opened 1998 and replaced the old Kai Tak one that jutted out into the bay from Kowloon.

She paused.

"Down in 15. Find a seat, and fasten those belts. A little gusty, they say."

In seconds both women were seated and buckled into the plush cabin seats. They'd learned to trust any and all observances and forecasts coming from Marli. Of the pilots out there flying spies around, she was one of the best.

• • •

As planned, Ling's imperial limo met them after a very abbreviated customs walk-through, whisking them off Lantau Island to the main island of Hong Kong, and then up Victoria Peak to the empress' palace.

They were met at the door by Yellow daughter, Empress Ling, and her young son, who would someday rule all of China.

Ling led them to the meeting room normally reserved for visiting diplomats, where they all took seats.

"Welcome to Hong Kong. Welcome to China. You can relax here, and put any jet lag into your recycle bin. Tomorrow, you'll be headed off to Ürümqi in Xinjiang. I believe you know that place well. Then, on to begin your Siberian quest. Since Xinjiang now has independence from China—one of my initial proclamations—I've arranged that you will enter what is essentially a new country with ease."

On cue, someone familiar entered through one of the gold-adorned archways.

Hekka and Phoebe both jumped to their feet, and rushed over to hug their favorite Uighur, Arzu.

Hekka was first to speak.

"It's been too long. And what are you doing here? I thought you were running Xinjiang."

Arzu smiled.

"I took the day off. Since we're newly independent, I wanted to make sure your entry at our Diwopu International Airport was without problem, and that those firearms you must carry make it through unnoticed. I'll do that for you."

"Thank you many times over, Arzu."

"You are welcome. We shall share a substantive Uighur dinner. Muslim tradition precludes alcohol with your meal, but somehow a nice bottle of wine might sneak in."

"Or a pitcher of Margaritas?"

Arzu laughed.

"I'll get you off to Siberia on time. Have a good night's sleep. There will be absolutely no drama while you're in my care. I promise."

"Well, then," Phoebe said. "Let's get our luggage off to our rooms, and get some grub."

She glanced around.

The luggage was gone.

"Oh. Sorry. My entourage, as they like to be called, is quite efficient."

• • •

They had a wonderful, authentic Chinese meal, parted for the night, and all parties slept fitfully.

Tomorrow was another day.

CHAPTER 17

That night, everyone slept fitfully in the sumptuous, palatial quarters atop Hong Kong's somewhat modified Victoria Peak.

The next morning, Yellow daughter entered room after room, opening drapes and letting the bright sun perform the alarm clock duties.

The guests, still rubbing their eyes, entered the reception room.

"C'mon, all," Ling cried out as she welcomed them first with a serene bow, and then with hand waves and a big smile.

She wore her classic black cheongsam dress, with all the gold embellishments, as a tribute to the old days when Hekka's husband, Mag Crayle, was in Hong Kong strategizing the overthrow and replacement of China's government.

"We're having breakfast out. At the Hard Rock!"

She witnessed stares of wonder.

"They'll open up early, just for me. We can chat, and then you need to be on your way. It's a long flight way out West to Xinjiang."

Hekka produced a 'wait a minute' look.

"I need Siberia, Ling. Not Xinjiang."

"It's just a stop. And I need you to return something. Someone, actually."

On cue, in through the gold-adorned archway walked someone both Hekka and Phoebe knew.

Arzu.

She stopped.

Bowed briefly.

"As I said, I'll get you into Xinjiang with no hassles. Then on to the Siberian wonderland."

• • •

All went well with breakfast at the Hard Rock. Hamburgers and eggs.

After a brief set of goodbyes, they were off in the Imperial limo to the airport, aboard the team's Dassault Falcon, buckled up, and in the air.

• • •

Once the jet was aloft, and all had settled in, Arzu unbuckled and addressed Hekka and Phoebe.

"I have something to play for you. Something Empress Ling asked me to do."

The other two looked intrigued. Attentive, they sat back to listen.

"She had me interview her. She knew I had some history as a reporter long ago. That's why she chose me. So, here goes."

She put her Smartphone on speaker, turned up the volume, and pressed PLAY.

"China's young leader, you, Empress Ling, decided to travel west to the Uighur province, Xinjiang. There you formally and personally acknowledged the province as a brand-new country and its, like you, young leader and friend, Arzu. The province and its people had been bequeathed to you by a sequence of events over the last few years as follows.

"First, the removal of the Maoist government by a small nuclear device. Next, the elevation of you to empress when the life of your husband, the new China Emperor Chin Yao-Wu, was taken.

"Normally you wouldn't leave the courtesan's and other plotters to their own devices by departing your Hong Kong palace. But you had someone you could trust. Yellow daughter would see to things for the few days you travelled. You would take along an appropriate entourage, including security on the advice of American President Kimbel Stones. He even loaned a Secret Service agent, fluent in Chinese, to ensure your safety. *Keep your friends close, and your enemies closer*, he'd said. Yes. The difficult ones would fill out her entourage. The specific Agent, Craig something or other, had experience protecting presidents and working out the details for visiting dignitaries and their own security people.

"Things went well from the start in Xinjiang. Yellow daughter received news that White daughter had given birth. You had to get back quickly lest someone declare White daughter the dowager empress to the newborn son and future emperor. Is that about right?"

Ling responded. "Close enough."

CHAPTER 18

Crayle would have preferred Phoebe at the wheel. Or himself. But she was off somewhere in Russia watching Hekka's back, and he had to process the Alpha Test version of the CIA's locator app. Team members in possession of the CIA Medallion would appear on a Google Maps lookalike screen. Something for the enemy neither to hack nor utilize. Alpha Test meant an organization used a new app internally before offering it to allies.

When Phoebe had taken her new ride, an ops-provided Porsche 911, that had survived their Monte Carlo operation, she'd gone the extra mile, so to speak. Porsche provided enthusiasts with lessons in an off-the-public-roads environment. She'd done well. And she'd provided husband and former SEAL, Micmac, with unofficial, white-knuckle instruction.

Micmac upgraded the docile Agency-provided Spanish SEAT. As he drove through central Funchal, the capitol of Portuguese Madeira Island, his skill level showed. Doing it behind the wheel of a brand new 911 Navy Blue Cabriolet put an indelible smile on his lips.

The pair headed uphill as did all who ventured inland into the precipitous topography of this East Atlantic island.

How the construction people got their equipment and materials up the near-vertical hills and built structures into crevices in the mountains surrounding Funchal remained a mystery. The villas pasted on the mountain side said that money—serious money—was involved.

As Micmac spun them up the hill with the mountain just right of their half of the one-and-a-half lane road, Crayle imagined the trip back with a 2,000 foot sheer drop boundary immediately on their right-hand side. And that depended on them surviving the meet arranged ahead at the end of the road. At the Eira do Serrado Hotel and Spa. If that went well, they'd check out the Terreiro da Luta with its famous Madonna and Child statue, and one helluva view out to sea. At least, that's what the intel said.

They reached the final curve. Micmac found a spot in the parking lot not relegated to the tour busses.

Just ahead, a souvenir shop and restaurant. Beyond, a path winding around the right side of a hundred-foot-high hill. Flagstone steps led to a lookout point around the curvature of the hill, not visible from their location. Micmac posted at the beginning of the inclined path where a series of steps began. Crayle ascended the 114 steps, taking care with the loosened flagstone that, with the drizzle that had just begun, provided pratfall potential.

He peered out over the walkway railing at the deep valley below. Two thousand feet down were the rooftops of quite a number of dwellings seemingly painted on the rolling valley floor. Across, high mountains poking into the clouds. Crayle proceeded with haste and caution up the 40 degree angle of the stairway to a viewing platform at the top.

With three tour busses parked below, it alerted Crayle to the absence of tourists at the lookout. Just one person there.

"Hi. I'm Rosanna," said the forty-ish woman. At 5'7", she didn't appear to pose a physical threat. Crayle knew better than to make such an assumption.

"*Bom dia*," he said in his best Portuguese.

"Good day right back," she responded with no accent.

Rosanna looked and sounded like a legitimate tour guide. No one suspected her long-term role as an ops officer with the Portuguese intelligence organization.

"I learned, Director Crayle, of your previous visit to our island, and your A Summit with the world's religious leaders. Congratulations."

"Thank you. There have been subsequent summits, and I hope we're past that. With the three religions leading, finally agreeing that Peace and Love must supplant War and Hate, we're heading in the right direction now."

"We have a population of German nationals here. They have their own ideas about who should run the world."

"So you've been read in regarding the Aryan Alliance."

"Portugal is not a backwater as some might believe. We know things."

Just then, a set of hang gliders appeared, skirting the mountains across the narrow valley. A mile or so away.

"Some people like to take their chances with the wind gusts and swirls of these volcanically-produced mountains," Rosanna informed. "It's a *rush* I believe you'd say in English."

"It would be if they weren't turning this way!"

• • •

He thought no one would attack him here because of his first World Peace Summit with the three religious leaders.

He was absolutely sure.

CHAPTER 19

Now back in Madeira Island's main town, Funchal, Crayle and Micmac parked the car, took to the sidewalk, and proceeded on foot.

Bordered by green mountains inland and cliffs to the East and West, nature seemed to have pushed the population out to the beautiful beaches and the Mediterranean Sea.

"I'm feeling good, my friend."

"I'm feeling it, too, Mag. Phoebs and I might just get a place here when we retire."

"What retire? I've got a run of four years on as DCI. So, request to retire anytime soon, denied."

"You know me. Like my SEAL mates past and present, I'm not a quitter."

"Amen to that. Hey, are you catching those aromas? Wafting through the air? Making me hungry."

"Me, too."

As if by magic, their assigned guide pulled up alongside.

"Please get in. I know a place."

• • •

The place was the restaurant, *Arazém do Sal.*

Inside, they had the sea bass specialty. It was delicious.

When they'd finished, and were ready to head back to their ship, the waitress handed them a bag.

"Your leftovers," she said.

Crayle glanced up at her.

"There was nothing left over."

"I was told that this bag was for you. Please take it. Or I will get in trouble."

Micmac took the bag, then tromped to their vehicle, and headed back to Funchal's cruise port, and their ship.

On the way, Crayle peeked into the bag.

Then, hoisted the contents.

It was a wood and metal treasure chest perhaps five inches by four, and three inches high.

He tried to flip open the lid, having noticed that the construction contained two silver metal hinges.

But, no.

"It's locked. Oh, well. We can get at it with your tool kit back in the stateroom."

• • •

Back in Micmac's room, they tried the tool set.

To no avail.

"Imagine that. Worst case, we cart it along and hand it to S & T when we get back to D.C."

"Then, we're outta here! On to Morocco!"

"High five!"

• • •

Somewhat farther to the East, in the New Persia, leaders proceeded through the initial stages of the new governance.

• • •

Rustom Modi sat in his office in his new palace. Here he was not only in his true homeland, but in the new capitol of a renamed empire. That the remodel had turned this spacious room into a lookalike of the American Oval Office made him smile. While relegated to Mumbai, India, as were his ancestors due to religious persecution, he came to enjoy the general nature of the Indian people. That he was Zoroastrian rather than Hindu didn't seem to bother them a bit. Live and let live seemed to translate nicely into their native Hindi language.

He glanced around. The Oval Office replica did have some local touches. The Americans did not revere ancient Persian leaders and have their portraits hung on the walls. These shared with replica Washington and Jefferson and their comrades, and there seemed to be a link.

Just then, the door burst open.

In strode Modi's wife, Leonor. Ambassador for the new Persia to the United Nations. As the Zoroastrian religion allowed for female priests, so did it allow them to represent Persia.

She was followed by Rustom's communications director.

"It's come, Your Highness! It's come!"

The ambassador gushed, and supplied additional punctuation. "It's official! The U.N. has officially disseminated throughout its bureaucracy our application. For nation status."

"My God," Modi replied. "The bureaucracy of all bureaucracies has come around. That means all references are now to Persia." He looked directly at the ambassador. "And references to the name, Iran?"

She gushed. "All deleted! Replaced!"

"Ah hum!"

They turned to the doorway.

"I couldn't help but hear the commotion. Being across the hall. So, the United Nations, which seldom gets things right, has spoken. It changes little. We are still and forever children of the One God. Of Allah."

Modi held up his hand.

"Listen to me, Grand Ayatollah. We are Persian children of the One God, now and forever. And your role, should you choose to accept it, or not, is to see that peace breaks out here in the Middle East. Then, the world. It's as our American friend, Mr. Crayle, has said. And so it shall be."

"I feel I'm in an episode of Mission Impossible, with due respect to Tom Cruise. *If I choose to accept it?*"

Modi reached for a remote, and punched in a code.

Out through the American Presidential JBL speakers blared the theme song for the iconic series.

They all smiled. Then, they laughed.

The Ayatollah broke into a dance that would've worked fine in a nineteen eighties disco.

The ambassador joined in.

Then, the comms director.

Then, Rustom Modi.

Peace seemed assured at this point. As Mag Crayle, the Magic Man, had ordained.

Persia's new political leader and the Muslim religious head were in sync.

They were with the beat.

CHAPTER 20

"Expect turbulence shortly, Mr. Lipschitz," Flori announced in her inimitable Brazil-sexy voice.

Back on one of the overstuffed seats, the P.I. ignored her.

Her next move with the Dassault Falcon business jet's joy stick resembled that of a video game expert.

Struggling, the whipsawed Lenny managed to click his seat belt.

As a direct consequence of the cabin video Flori watched with a smile, the 'turbulence' subsided to zero.

"Fasten seat belts," she said.

The Falcon 8X set down at the Prince Edward Island's Charlottetown Airport with no further ado.

"You may unfasten your seat belt, now."

Lenny did, grabbed his official CIA-certified Go Bag, and deplaned.

A car awaited. It's driver, a petite redhead, stepped out to take his luggage, plop it into the trunk, and introduce herself.

"Hi, I'm Anne. Anne Green is my maiden name."

Lenny didn't typically make friends right away.

"It's not likely that you are a maiden," he adlibbed. "Your last name is Gables."

"How did you guess? Anne Green Gables. From Cavendish. We're headed there now."

They departed Charlottetown in short order, headed across the narrow width to the long island's East coast. Lenny would have to wait to check out the wonders of the PEI Canadian province's capitol city. Right now, it was business only.

• • •

The pair headed across the narrow part of PEI to the farm site of Green Gables fame.

Ann walked them past the *Closed for Maintenance* sign. The front door was not locked.

Lenny followed her inside.

As farmhouses went, Green Gables was pretty standard.

The furniture seemed real and ancient—no modern materials—and, of course, there was a substantive fireplace with real wood stacked nearby.

"Come, Lenny," she said, which seemed a common repartee for the women he'd known.

He followed her upstairs to a comfy-looking room with a large wooden desk.

The petite redhead plopped down in the high back chair. She pointed at the top right drawer.

"We're not supposed to open these, but today is special … and, yes, you are my special guest."

Lenny was not at all a shy person.

He complied.

What stared back at him right there in front and on top was yet another metal and wood treasure chest.

He just stared for a few seconds. Then, he picked it up. And shook it.

"Sounds the same as the others. So, number three."

"We'll go have some islander food, Lenny. I know just the place. Then, we're off to somewhere new. New for you, that is."

Her enduring smile had him. As did her long, red braids. He placed the new treasure chest in his backpack with the others, and off they went.

The kidnapping of Lenny Lipschitz came off as if scripted.

He'd have a talk with Darryl.

CHAPTER 21

The three men who'd kidnapped Lenny strapped him into the cockpit and closed the canopy lid, assuring that it was securely latched. Having it pop open at 300 miles per hour would not bode well for their captive, whom they seriously needed as well as their associate in the back seat. The two men remaining outside the vehicle stood ready.

All complete, the leader waved his arm and ordered, "*Los!*"

The 'let it go!' in German was all that was needed for his colleague to flip the switch using the subterranean transport app. The two of them would follow in a second cockpit.

The vehicle, 300 feet beneath the surface of Prince Edward Island, motored forward, the airlock doors opening and then closing behind.

As soon as the operational vacuum was achieved, the capsule accelerated as fast as the two humans inside could withstand.

Just minutes later, deceleration commenced. The vehicle came to a stop.

Lenny caught his breath.

Besides being a captive, he had the additional problem of having heard the men—the ones left behind—discussing a giant boring machine facing from PEI and set to bore to the East toward Nova Scotia's Cape Breton Island. The cochlear implant in Lenny's ear translated the German in real time.

Lenny would warn Darryl, if he lived long enough.

After he was extracted from the cockpit, his captors interrogated him regarding Crayle's whereabouts as the man and his team represented a threat to the Aryan Alliance.

With a special command, Lenny could turn off the verbal translation but he kept it on. He realized that the language spoken, German, indicated that his captives were of the Aryan Alliance and remembered the impediments to their dreams of fulfilling Adolph Hitler's quest for world conquest and domination that the Crayle team had already delivered. That they were responsible for his kidnapping spoke volumes. They might be down, but definitely not out.

Lenny's new red-haired friend, Anne, appeared on the scene in the next instant.

With deadly accuracy, she shot Lenny's captors dead.

She took out her Smartphone.

She turned to him.

"I'll have to call for help."

She waited.

"Cleanup on aisle three."

• • •

Topside at Chicoutimi there stood a pulp house. A sign said so. It symbolized that longstanding effort to process the extensive forestry into paper products, to be shipped all over the world.

They reached the pulp house in under a half hour.

Lenny had a question for his guide.

"So, what's your real name? Your first name?"

"I don't have one."

"That can't be. Everyone has a first name. Also called a given name."

"My parents couldn't think of one … that they agreed on. So that space was left blank on the live birth certificate."

"I'll just call you Blank, then."

She laughed. Alone.

"I'm not sure you have much of a sense of humor, Lenny."

"I've heard that before." He frowned.

She pointed. "There's the pulp building over there."

He saw it. A three-story building that looked like 1800s architecture.

He followed her to a door on the second level, then inside.

The pulp house interior was cavernous. The only floor they could see was about fifteen feet below at the ground level. With nothing but a roll-top desk and two chairs.

Just inside the door, they stood on a four-by-four landing. A long steel stairway led down. Another led up.

He followed her, stepping carefully, then over to the desk.

His guide took a seat and popped open the roll-top.

Nothing, except a small wood and metal treasure chest. A duplicate of those he'd acquired in Nova Scotia and Prince Edward Island.

Just then, a sound from above.

Up at the third level, a giant iron cauldron hung suspended by large knobs on either side.

"The raw pulp goes into that vessel. Then, they stream it to that big receptacle on the bottom floor. The process smoothes out the pulp as it homogenizes it. So there are not thick spots and thin spots. All the same."

Then, another noise.

They looked up.

There, standing on a platform to the side of the cauldron, stood a tall, solidly built man. A blond haired man. He peered down at them, then walked a couple of feet to a wall-mounted control panel, and pulled gently on a protruding, wooden lever.

The floor slid sideways, apparently accommodated by a slot cut into the adjacent hillside.

Lenny and Anne jumped from the retreating floor onto a metal receptacle that encompassed the entire bottom of the building.

They looked up.

The blond man pulled another lever.

The cauldron began to tilt.

A narrow stream of steaming hot pulp fell the two stories landing just a few feet from the pair.

Quick, Lenny reached inside his jacket and extracted his stainless steel Walther PPK.

Anne poked her hand into purse end slot, pulling out an identical, but European-blued, arm.

Their assailant grabbed the lever to pull it wide open just as they fired.

Both shots struck his upper torso.

He wobbled, then fell into the partially tipped cauldron of steaming pulp.

He disappeared.

Another quick, but well-aimed, shot by Anne struck the lever, knocking it upward.

The cauldron ceased its dribbling, and returned to its normal inactive position.

Lenny grabbed her hand, pulling her toward the stairway.

"Wait! Don't forget your treasure chest!"

He yanked off his backpack and pulled the zipper.

She told him the reason for the trip here.

The treasure chest.

• • •

Lenny zipped up and repositioned the pack, took Anne's hand once more, and led her to the stairs. Twenty seconds later, they reached the landing, and he pulled her through the doorway into fresh air.

"I heard him yell out something as he pulled that second lever," Lenny said.

"Yes. I heard. Of all things, it was in German."

"What?"

"*Fertig*. It means *finished*."

"Well, Charles Darwin won another one."

"You mean, *survival of the fittest*?"

"You're saying you're one of the fittest?"

"No. And that's what worries me."

• • •

His guide drove him by what looked a lot like the pyramid at the Parisian Louvre.

"You'll like this, Lenny," she said. "It's called the Ha! Ha! Pyramid."

Then, she laughed.

"What so funny about that, eh?"

The 'eh' at the end was typical Canadian English, according to Lenny's experiences in the vast land. It seemed to correspond to an American adding 'right?" to the end of a statement. Most times, it was rhetorical. No response necessary or expected.

"The Ha! Ha! Pyramid commemorates the great flood of 1996 … eh."

"After a great flood, I would've come up with the same thing," Lenny responded sarcastically.

"We need to get to Quebec City," Anne said. "Now!"

He glanced around at the magnificent, remote scenery of the Saguenay fjord. "I suppose you can hotwire seaplanes, or have a kite stowed in that man-sized purse of yours."

"Come with me."

She latched onto his hand and practically dragged him along. Back to their point of ingress. The porta potty.

She opened the door, and waved him inside.

He complied, but not without comment.

"I'm getting really tired of plucking out short and curlies for ID. If it weren't for Alona, I'd have you do it."

"If I did it, it would hurt. Really, really bad."

Their ID's validated, in seconds they were back beneath the Earth.

"Over here." Anne motioned to another cockpit. It sat astride rails that headed Southwest.

"That's the way to Quebec City. Let's give it a shot."

They repeated the process that got them from Prince Edward Island to Saguenay in the first place. Into the airlock and up to 300 miles per hour.

The entirety of the trip lasting but a few minutes took them under the Saint Lawrence River, terminating deep below Quebec City.

Lenny checked his phone for intel.

"Let's see, Quebec City founded 1608 by somebody named Champlain. Has just over 500,000 folks. British held it from 1759 'til 1763. Back and forth with the French for a while. Then, France gave it to the Brits in 1763. It bears an Algonquin indigenous name, meaning *where the river narrows*. As if I didn't know that. On top is a plateau with a citadel and the world-class Chateau Frontenac hotel where Churchill and Roosevelt plotted the World War II D-Day incident. Got it."

An elevator ride up to the porta potty found them in the *Jardin des Gouverneurs*. The Garden of the Governors occupied a special city block. A short walk to the north end of the park and across its boundary street found them at the *Manoir Vieux Quebec*—the Old Quebec Manor. It operated as a hotel with several rooms on each of its three floors, plus a city view platform up on top.

Their prime location sat equidistant between the world-renowned Chateau Frontenac and the city's ancient, star-shaped citadel.

They'd spend the night.

CHAPTER 22

It didn't matter that she was driving down 'Main Street' of a major, ancient Siberian city. The motorists and pedestrians of the Lake Baikal mainstay, Irkutsk, fully appreciated her ride. Hekka Crayle sat behind the wheel of a fully restored 1962 Chevrolet Impala. Dark with a lipstick red interior. It was coincidence that the red matched the aggressive shade worn by pilot Marli, whose overt Hollywood style sunglasses also matched the vehicle's style.

Beside her, riding shotgun, sat her new local guide so full of local intel Hekka would have to give special thanks to Ling for setting this up.

Yes. Ling. Empress of China.

Hekka had it on good authority, from the National Security Agency, that this very car had cruised Hollywood's renowned Sunset Boulevard in the years, '66 and '67, even during the protests that generated the iconic Buffalo Springfield tune, *For What It's Worth*.

In the back seat, replete with smiles, sat Phoebe, her protector and Czarina Anastasia's number one, Raspi.

Each rider had a 'don't try this at home' ear piece, allowing clear, in car, near field comms on trial from the CIA's Science and Technology Directorate. Especially with the Chevy's convertible top down.

They drove back and forth until Raspi spotted a Starbucks.

"Be careful with the driving. Don't want to run over any of those Communist exiles out here."

"What's that all about, Raspi?"

"After MAD—Mutually Assured Destruction—became real in the 1970s, the Communist need to destroy America didn't go away. Gorbachev's Perestroika switched us from overt to covert Commies."

"That way, by destroying the U.S. from within, there would be no retaliation as would have been from a nuclear strike."

"Right."

"But Anastasia got all the former Communists to Red Square when she repatriated Vladimir's body. Then, she had the mini-nuke hidden in his coffin go off, thus eliminating the threat of that party making a comeback.

"But the few that were so bad they were exiled to Siberia … here … didn't make the pilgrimage to Moscow for the funeral. They're still here somewhere."

"Do they have a following?"

"That's like asking if a skunk has a following."

"Then, they're not a danger to anyone."

"They'll just live in peace, enjoy all the capitalism that goes on in Siberia, and be gone someday."

CHAPTER 23

"Too bad Lenny couldn't make this run," Phoebe said while she regarded her nails.

"You'll not win any sincerity award for that statement."

"I know. I feel awful."

"Hey, tango approaching our heading. 035."

The FBI Agent leaned in.

"Oh! Talk dirty, Hekka!"

"Hi," the mid-sized, 5' 7" woman said as she drew near enough to speak softly and be understood. With her was a thin man, slightly taller and garbed in a saffron robe.

"This is Miao-Yin. He's a for real Buddhist, but has critical knowledge and contacts we'll need on our journey." Strangely, he wore an American sports team emblem on his tunic. It appeared to be a New Orleans Saints logo.

"Hello, Miao-Yin. I'm Hekka. H-E-K-K-A. This is Phoebe. P-H-O-E-B-E."

Clearly, the man appeared puzzled. How could an English word starting with P sound like one that began with F? Perhaps the fish he'd heard of was spelled phlounder.

"I am a certified Buddhist. Do not be surprised when lay persons of the order give me food. It is customary. In turn, I pray for their souls."

"Mmm," Phoebe noted. "Food for everlasting life. Not a bad trade."

The cleric appeared a bit miffed by her remark.

Ever the peacemaker, Hekka assisted. "We'll forego any more religious references. We don't wish to upset you."

Phoebe added, "Really good that Lenny's not here."

The memory of turning a peaceful group of Buddhists into a bloodthirsty mob at their recent sojourn in the Chinese Xinjiang province came to mind.

"Where do you live, Miao-Yin?"

"Across the lake. Baikalsk. Near Ulan-Ude. Our territory is Eastern Siberia. I know the place quite well."

He said that as if he was trying to prove his worth to the point of being a nuisance.

Hekka hoped not. There was enough to do without distractions.

CHAPTER 24

Crayle initiated a memory test. He'd been to Rabat and Casablanca before. He appreciated the anticipated lack of violence this go round.

"The French had occupied Casablanca. They'd imposed a protectorate with the Treaty of Fès, 1912. They already had an imperial presence in Algeria and Tunisia. A division of all Morocco between France and Spain was terminated by the United Nations. In modern days, Rabat served as the national capitol of Morocco. Contradictions battled with diversity for purchase. Rabat was positioned Northeast up the Atlantic Coast from the city of Bogart and Bergman Hollywood fame. Rabat contained an ancient walled shopping area—the medina.

"The city was reputed to possess two of Morocco's best museums. The *Musée de l'Histoire et des Civilisations* and the Mohammed VI Museum of Modern and Contemporary Art. Morocco's North Atlantic coast guested Phoenicians, Romans, Portuguese, Spanish in much of its history. It even served as ancient pirate Sale's stronghold, with the town Asilah reflecting the look and feel of Southern Spain,

Andalusian style. In Casablanca, the Hassan II mosque, with its art-deco architecture, is today the only mosque allowing non-Muslim visits. I ate at La Koutoubia, founded in 1955, I believe, and highly recommend it."

"Brings to mind an old tune I played," Micmac inserted. "*Rock the Casbah*."

"A casbah is a fortified dwelling, by the way."

His colleague and spy associate smiled at the memory recall.

"The seventh century brought the arrival of Islam. The Almoravids from 1062 until 1147. And, from the high mountains inland, the Almohads from 1121 'til 1269. They displaced the increasingly decadent Almoravids. Then they took over all of Morocco and Spanish Andalusia. The Almohads cherished enlightenment, but were not zealots like their predecessors.

"They created a great economy, founded universities that produced a flourishing intellectual life. There was unequaled splendor. That was the good news. They were driven from Andalusia by the Spanish Christian princes, and their civilization descended into a period of revolutionary nomads taking power from corrupt city dwellers, only to become bloated and complacent themselves."

"It seems to be the human condition, Mag."

"Yeah. A guy named Sidi Mohammed Ben Abdullah established Rabat as the capitol. He stuck around between 1757 until 1790. Rabat became the political capitol of Morocco in 1912."

"That's quite a history. When we get back, we need to meet with President Stones, have him make Lenny the ambassador here."

"Great idea, Micmac. We've been at peace with Morocco too darn long. Send Lenny as ambassador. That'll fix things."

CHAPTER 25

Ali was not the standard CIA operational asset with tour guide employment as cover. In fact, he was not yet a tour guide. He served for all to see as a tour guide's assistant. It wasn't clear if the actual Moroccan guide was an asset, or was employed without his knowledge as an asset.

Today's tour for Crayle and Micmac debarked their Island Princess cruise ship in Casablanca.

To avoid contact with other of the ship's passengers, they'd docked on a pier dedicated to container ships. A giant crane hovered over a very special container.

Machine Parts listed on its manifest left out a few details. Details such as sidearms, plus carbines capable of full-automatic fire.

And a few shrink-wrapped packets of C-4 explosives.

The downside was it required a half-mile walk from the ship to the port-exit building and the waiting tour bus.

Ali noted that this was a special sailing for a special mission. Someone could have picked the Celebrity Cruise Lines due to the lookalike fake celebs on board.

Everyone went by their given first names, or their nickname—no last names were used. None were needed.

Mick J., Ronnie W., Tom F., Eric C., Crayle team spy musician Mick M., and the manager, Mag C.

They were all there.

When the final two, Micmac and Crayle, departed, the latter used a cane. It was hard to keep up with the others.

Crayle and Micmac lagged behind.

Part of Ali's job was to stay back, ensuring that laggards didn't get lost from the tour group. Being a foreigner with no local language skills, no emergency contacts, and little or no foreign currency would leave a tourist stranded. Not good for publicity and marketing, or for public image of a cruise line or a tour company.

The lagging Crayle and Ali had a chance to make contact with their transportation, while legitimate tourists surged ahead.

• • •

"We're set for dinner at a little place in Casablanca. Then, back to the ship to sleep it off."

"Micmac, this is a Muslim country. Getting toasted means a big fire, and medium- well to well done."

"They are accommodating here … and you are channeling Lenny's sense of humor. Again."

He waited a beat.

"Relax, Mag. I've got this."

He said something unintelligible to the driver. Then, translated for his fellow spy.

"We're stopping off near the main drag. Named after Almohad."

Micmac checked out a street sign.

"There you go. We're getting close."

The nature of espionage was consistent in at least one way. When you felt sure of something, or someone, in the next minute you weren't.

"And where did you pick up the Arabic?"

"Oh, it's nothing really. Just a short session with ole Doc Rorschach. Not enough to do much with."

"Like read street signs written in Arabic script."

"Moroccan script, actually. But, yeah."

Their driver and guide, Ali, pulled in and parked at the establishment.

Rick's Café.

As they stepped inside, it was as Crayle remembered.

The café tables and chairs, the waiters, and even the dulcet tones of Sam's piano.

Seated, Micmac took the lead. He placed their order. In Arabic.

"I ordered the Champagne Oysters to get started. And the Goat Cheese with figs. Then, the Char-Grilled Ribeye. We'll finish with Rick's Cheesecake."

"Sounds good," Crayle said as he continued to survey the room. "I can't wait if that's what you ordered in Arabic."

"Regarding the Arabic. If you'd been watching me instead of scanning for Humphrey Bogart and Ingrid Bergman, you'd have seen me point things out on the menu. Okay?"

• • •

The meal was just past fabulous.

Relaxation was really setting in. Micmac closed it off.

"Oh, waiter?"

The waiter stepped over, and handed a paper bag to the sailor.

"From the bar. Two dry vodka martinis. With those fabulous Moroccan olives. And shaken, not stirred."

• • •

Later, on boarding their ship, Crayle expressed his appreciation to Micmac for taking time away from home to help him get himself back together.

“My pleasure. Really. Oh, and here’s your leftover carton in the bag. You’ll want to check it out before you heat it up.”

Crayle took the bag, and headed to his stateroom.

Curious, he lifted the cardboard box from the bag, and opened it.

There, before him, was not the remains of the fabulous meal. No. It was a box made of dark-stained wood, with silver metal hinges, and a lock. He extricated the chest, previously obtained in Madeira, from his room safe, and set it next to the new one.

The same in every respect.

“What,” he said out loud, “is going on?”

CHAPTER 26

The cockpit-like vehicle sailed through the vacuum-enabled tube. In seconds, Lenny and his guide transited from the Saguenay River port to a place about 100 miles West. Or 150 kilometers.

Quickly topside into the town called Beaupré, she led him to their transportation. A moderate size silver sedan.

"Get in, Lenny. Driver side."

"Why don't you drive? You know the area. And the laws. The crazy French-Canadian drivers and I don't get along."

She produced a serious shake of her head.

"Get in. Buckle up."

He did. He glanced at her. "Well?"

She touched an app on her Canadian intelligence agency Smartphone. Then she tapped a preset icon.

The car jumped forward from the curb as if electric. It was.

With no input from 'driver' Lenny, it sped, it braked, and it turned.

At traffic lights, a high-definition screen between the two passengers counted down as if the traffic system had been hacked.

"It's run by AI. You know, artificial intelligence?"

"What do I do?"

"Sit there, and relax."

At zero on the screen, the light changed. The rabid acceleration shoved them hard against the seat backs.

With no say in the matter, the two were rushed out of town and on to a two-lane country road, headed North. Minutes later, their self-driving vehicle pulled up to a small building.

Inside, a clerk directed them to a golf-cart-like vehicle pointed at a narrow dirt road.

"Oh, no!" Lenny waved his arms. "Oh, no!"

"It's okay." The guide nodded to their right. "She'll drive."

A young woman approached.

"Lenny, this is Anne de Beaupré. She'll drive."

He turned, and stared at her long, red braids.

"That's not Anne de Beaupré! That's Anne of Green Gables. From Prince Edward Island!"

"Actually," said the young and petite redhead with a smile, "I'm Sainte Anne de Beaupré, too."

Lenny pushed his lips to one side, a characteristic of his wife, Alona.

Then, "You've been promoted. You know, the saint thing?"

"C'mon. Get in. I drive good."

"Y'know, Sainte Anne. After this trip, someone's gonna make me a saint, too."

No one would take the odds against that eventuality to Las Vegas.

• • •

Five minutes later, Anne delivered them to a copse of trees. The benches there presaged an overlook to the river below. And a foot bridge ahead.

Anne spoke. "Lenny, go on ahead. There's something for you on the bridge that overlooks the falls. It's only a couple of hundred feet above the river. So, should be a cakewalk for an experienced private investigator."

Lenny's P.I. experiences taught him to worry whenever someone downplayed the experience ahead.

He walked the path anyway.

Twenty seconds later he arrived at the West end of the bridge.

Some bridge.

It was strung across the river gorge, held up by two cables which doubled as hand rails. The walking portion dangled a couple of feet below the cables. And the walkway was a two-foot-wide span of wooden boards, hopefully affixed somehow to the bridge. The whole thing appeared to be about 100 feet long.

He took three steps.

And stopped.

With the second step, the bridge began to bounce.

Lenny was not a large or heavy man. Nice people called him diminutive.

Down a foot, rebounding up a foot.

A two foot bounce.

He knew it wouldn't get any better as he progressed away from Mother Earth.

So, he tiptoed.

The bridge didn't care. Twenty steps in, it oscillated at least three feet. Up and down.

Thirty steps, four feet.

He held on to the suspension cables at either side as if his life depended on it.

When he stopped for a second and looked down, he was sure it did.

"That's at least a thousand feet down! Sainte Anne … lied!"

All was not lost.

Just a few feet farther lay a bag taped to the foot boards.

Lenny proceeded. With one hand, he secured the bag.

In slow motion, he let go of the rail with his other hand, and opened it.

"Well I'll be damned. Another treasure chest. Just like the other four."

With great care not to move any more than absolutely necessary, he stuffed it in his backpack.

Just then, he heard a commotion at the far end of the bridge.

Eight high-school-aged boys had stepped on, and one started jumping.

Then, more.

Then, all eight.

The bridge went into fibrillation mode.

Six feet up, six feet down.

Lenny held on for dear life. Maybe Anne of whatever was less than a saint than she claimed.

Something new.

A tall well-built man with blond hair forced his way through the teenager scrum, yelling at them in a foreign language.

The boys yelled back in their native French.

He got through, and broke into a run, his eyes fixated on Lenny.

With outstretched arms, the assailant was about to leap at the much smaller P.I.

But the high schoolers recovered from the one man onslaught.

They started to jump, ensemble, more vigorously than before.

The blond man lost his balance, and plunged over the rail.

Yelling "*Scheisse!*"—the German word for excrement.

Lenny backed off the foot bridge, made it to the copse of trees and stumbled over to the ladies breathless.

Anne hugged him tight.

"I'm sorry, Lenny," she said. "I didn't see that coming at all. I may need to hand in my halo."

"It's alright. I'm alive, and I got the prize. Let's jump on that golf cart, and blow this joint."

They did just that.

On the automated ride back—less exhilarating than the suspension foot bridge—back to Beaupré, the guide apprized the P.I. of what came next.

"We're back to our subterranean two-person bullet train, and off to Quebec City. Just relax. Take it easy. You're almost done."

"I feel almost dead."

"Relax."

CHAPTER 27

At a speed in excess of one hundred miles per hour, Anne and Lenny made the underground 'flight' from Sainte Anne de Beaupré in minutes.

The canopy popped open. Lenny extracted himself, with a tug of the hand from his young, red haired spy-guide. With a wave, he gladly bade farewell to this mode of transportation.

Everything about the station looked familiar. He concluded, he'd been here before.

Up they went to the surface, using a special bathroom stall. It was blocked off from the others with a permanent *Closed for Maintenance* sawhorse in front of its door.

As the two exited, they drew knowing glances and smiles from the few women at the sinks.

Outside, he followed her lead to the curb.

In short order, a car pulled up, looking suspiciously like the one at Sainte Anne. And, likewise, without a driver.

"Oh, no!" Lenny'd had enough of the white knuckle mode of transport.

"C'mon, Len. We'll hop in the back. You know. Fool around."

"Fool around? You're Sainte Anne."

"I've seen your look. You want some."

"They must've lowered the bar for sainthood."

"Backstory. Early on, I decided to serve the One God everyone was talking about. I entered a convent. It didn't go well. There was this priest. Got to know me in the biblical sense."

Lenny's face went blank.

"I got bounced out … and became a spy. I mean, what's a girl to do?"

He understood a rhetorical question when he heard one.

"C'mon, Lenny. We'll zip over to the Manoir Vieux-Quebec, and screw away the rest of the afternoon."

"I'm faithful, Anne. End of story. There'll be no knowledge, biblical or otherwise."

Unexpectedly, she smiled.

Then, she tapped her right ear bud.

"Did you get that?"

She listened, and turned to Lenny.

"She got that."

Then, "Alright, Alona. Anne out."

Lenny gasped.

"She was listening the whole time? Not possible. We went dark when I started this thing in Sydney, Nova Scotia."

"Sweetheart, you are doing this as a private investigator, not a spy, There is no dark. Besides, these are burner ear buds. And encrypted. No one can hear us. And if they can, then it's garbled."

Without further drama, their car pulled up in front of the Manoir. The two were out, inside, checked in, and up to their room in five minutes.

Anne pulled out the ear buds. She placed them in a STIC—Sound and Technology Isolated Container.

She turned to Lenny, sporting a smile too wicked even for a redhead of her young age.

"Let's do it, hon. Over and over. Like putting it in the bank so you can abstain later on … for Alona."

"Your sense of humor is … well … like mine. Not funny."

"That you recognized it as humor earns you a Sainte Anne point."

She reached out.

"And with that, we head upstairs to the top deck. There's something you need to see."

• • •

Outside the room, they took the stairway to the top of the building, and stepped outside.

They were treated to a great view on a beautiful, clear day.

Anne led him around the stairway structure to a table and two chairs.

Lenny felt he'd been here before. Or perhaps Mag had told him about it.

He wondered how his boss, and friend, was coming along with his memory regurgitation.

His thoughts were interrupted due to a quick move by the young woman.

Her hand flew under the table, ripped something and its attendant duct tape out, and set the item on the table.

"Treasure chest number six, Lenny. But you're not finished. After we do, or don't do, stuff back in the room, you're to take your back pack and the six items to the airport.

• • •

"I'll fetch a ride for you. Or us."

"To which hell and gone place am I going this time?"

"Surprise, surprise. Your heading Northwest. A little burg in the Yukon Territory. It's called Dawson City."

"I believe I've been there."

"There, as you put it, is where all shall be revealed."

"I did some research before I headed out on this insane trip. Canada has ten provinces, and three territories. The Yukon is the West most of the territories. Right next to Alaska."

"Well, unless you want to get serious here on this bed, let's get going. I'll notify your pilot, Flori, that we're on the way."

"You mean the same hyper-sexual Flori that I know? In the non-biblical sense, of course?"

"You are just surrounded by sexy women. Maybe someday you'll get lucky."

"I already got lucky. With Alona."

"I heard that," emanated from the STIC.

CHAPTER 28

"So sorry to hear about your father, Vladimir's, death. Being returned to Moscow, laid to final rest next Comrade Lenin, then blown sky high with one of those mini-nuclear devices. Such desecration."

"It was he, my father, who exiled me to Siberia."

The other man was feeling a bit uncomfortable at the unexpected response.

"I didn't know."

"Still, you were right. It was painful to hear, and any chance to reconcile, gone."

"I'm betting it was the Czarina. No proof, but she benefitted when our colleagues in Communism swarmed from all over to Red Square and were obliterated."

"Obliterated? A fancy English word for a Russian."

"Spent my undergrad years in Santa Barbara. The University of California institution."

"Another fancy word. One you might use just once in your remaining years."

The other man hadn't survived this long with the ruthless man admonishing him with sparsely veiled threats by snapping back. His response was tactical.

"I shall keep that in mind."

"Yes. I believe it was the Ukrainians. The felt they owed us one big one for the invasion of their country. They blamed my father for all the deaths and destruction."

"We'll deal with them later. First, we must terminate the American menace that so cleverly caused the destruction of our party's Soviet Union. I plan to capture the one who's come here for research. This Hekka Crayle. That should draw in the rest of them. When we have them all, we shall kill them. Perhaps feed their bodies to the sturgeon in the Caspian."

"So what do we know about the American spy crew?"

"We know names, locations, mostly, and back stories."

"I'm impressed. And how do we know so much about the darkest of America's spy resources?"

"You might have guessed the Dark Web."

"Or perhaps, the Darkest Web."

"Neither one. Our man in the Aryan Alliance provided that intel."

"A German? How many times in history has a German actually helped a Russian?"

"The list would be brief. But it is to their benefit that we take out the American Crayle team. So, our interests coalesce."

"Coalesce? I need a drink. A local vodka. No vermouth. No anything else. Shaken. Not stirred."

"Spoken like a true Russian spy. So shall it be."

CHAPTER 29

There they were. Just ahead on the Lena River lay Yakutsk with a population of 312,000, just East of the Siberian center. Here, the Lena River headed due North many miles to the Laptev Sea. In the Arctic Ocean.

They were set to meet a local to check out ancient migrant artifacts, and then get themselves headed East to the Chukchi Peninsula. Siberia's easternmost aspect. Just a Bering Strait width from America's biggest state. Alaska.

"Hi, there. Thanks for your help. My name is Hekka."

"Oh," the 30-something woman responded. "My name is also Hekka."

"I'm not buying coincidence here," said the on-loan FBI Special Agent. Phoebe's hand moved slowly to her lower back. And her .45 caliber Glock 30.

"No, my name is actually Phoebe."

She waited for a light-hearted, ice broken response.

"Hey," the real Phoebe interjected. "Do we wait around for you to be Alona, or can we get on with things?"

"Czarina Anastasia told me to say that. She said it would be joke."

Her warm smile caused Phoebe to ease off a tad.

"Yes. She chose me to ensure that you could trust me, and to assist with the local dialects of the Yakut people. Now, to artifacts. And to get you on your way East."

She paused to insure that all was understood.

"Yes, we get on with things. The canoe will be taken care of. When we finish here in Yakutsk, I take you to your ride to Chukchi Peninsula. Over the two mountain ranges East. There you will be met by ... Alona ... who will take you rest of way."

• • •

Hekka and Phoebe, tired from their long journey on the Lena River, homed in on the Yakutsk Starbucks. They'd catch a coffee with a large infusion of caffeine. Then, to the McDonalds across the road. So much for sampling local fare.

They picked an outside table and sat down just as a man approached. With one hand on their coffee cups and one not far from their lower-back holsters, they watched.

"Hello, Mrs. Crayle and Mrs. MacKay. I am Ilya Kuriakin. I am assigned to help you find—how you say—artifacts from long ago."

It was not lost on Phoebe that one of her dearly departed dad's favorite TV shows from long ago was I Spy.

Yes, a spy story. And Ilya Kuriakin was a Soviet spy played by one David McCallum.

Aziza and Arzu, it turns out, were needed back in Xinjiang and Uzbekistan. They'd left. To Hekka and Phoebe's ultimate surprise, who walked out the Starbucks door to where they sat?

One Kianna Tarni. The one for whom Hekka had named her first-borne. The aboriginal operative from the Australian Intelligence Service, who'd saved their lives in what seemed like the long ago.

"I will accompany you to Chukchi and beyond."

Why not?

Why not have an aboriginal spy from the down under help them in far Eastern Siberia? On a mission of indigenous people research.

Who better?

Why not?

CHAPTER 30

Back on the cruise ship, the alarm went off at 6 A.M.

The only question was which one of the quickly drawn .40 caliber SIG-Sauers was going to end its misery.

Crayle and Micmac shared a laugh.

"And I'm supposed to relax," said Crayle.

"Yeah. Let's get out of here, grab some grub, and then off to our restful excursion … on the pier at 7."

"There is no restful at 7. Restful would be around noon. Or later."

"C'mon, Mag. Rise and shine. We'll check out the wonderful and beauteous port of Malaga, Spain from the buffet topside."

Within a half hour, they were doing just that.

"Spice this meal up, Mag. Test your mind some more. Give me some intel."

"Between bites. Will do."

He consumed the better part of an over medium egg, and went into lecturer mode.

"What you see out there is a parenthetical bay. Left and right parens enclose the harbor. The flats ahead give way inland to hills. We'll see tile and cobblestone walkways. There's a domed white building that serves as a safe house."

"Wait a minute. How do you know it's a safe house?"

"Been here, done that."

He waited a couple of beats for that to sink in.

"There are carriage and horse rides if we feel ambitious. Orange-spoked wheels on black carriages. White horses, mostly. There's a twenty-story downtown with shorter structures around that. And a circular, multi-tiered bull ring, if you're feeling brave. And how about a wide beach with dark, moist sand."

"Sounds good. And … it's time to go."

They left the buffet, gathered their purple, numbered excursion group stickers, and were down on the pier in short order. There, they met their guide for the day.

"Hi," said the pretty, statuesque blond woman. "I'm your guide, Kristine. Follow me."

Crayle noticed the German accent, but said nothing. He was to relax.

She led them to a black van with darkened windows. They headed through Malaga just like so many tourists before them.

"Our town is capitol of the Province of Malaga, which is within the Spanish territory, Andalusia."

"We've been to this area before," said Crayle. He left out the overbaked scheme of Portuguese and Spanish master villains, and their enablers, the Aryan Alliance from Germany.

"We have just under 600,000 residents in our great city. And we have history. About 2,800 years. Looking to the future, our city has become a technology hub. We have the Málaga TechPark."

"Then you Malaguenans have a bright future"

"You used that term, Mr. Crayle. Do you know of the song?"

Micmac jumped in. "I'm a guitarist, Kristine. I learned the Malagueña early on. I really got to love Flamenco music."

The van pulled over.

"It is time for our walking portion of the tour."

Kristine opened the passenger side sliding door.

Before they could alight, a young girl, perhaps four years old, appeared at the doorway.

She smiled broadly.

"*Aqui, Señor*. This is for you."

He wasn't sure how to react.

Relax, his mind said.

He took what looked to be a small, wood and metal treasure chest. Just like the ones he'd received on Madeira and in Morocco. He looked up.

The girl smiled again, then turned and ran down the sidewalk.

He turned to Micmac.

"It appears that everyone in the world thinks I'm a secret agent."

"It seems everyone in the world *knows* you're a secret agent."

Crayle only had one question.

What in the world was going on?

CHAPTER 31

The zodiac containing some of their enemies had trouble getting permission to exit Malaga harbor. That allowed Crayle and Micmac to convince the captain of the Island Princess cruise ship to crank the engines, drop shore power, and pursue its scheduled course Northeast to Cartagena. A bit early.

Passengers on sponsored tours would be transported to the next port at cruise line expense. Those on private tours—good luck.

The zodiac got its permission and headed out—restricted by the 5 km/hour harbor speed limit.

With the cruise ship in pursuit.

Out of the harbor, the somewhat terrified enemies went full ahead on their outboard engines, manufactured by Mercury, apparently the god of speed.

By now, Crayle and Micmac stood alone on the bow's main deck, the former SEAL bedecked in a well-worn-in diver suit. Crayle helped him don a chest-borne rebreather, two side-worn tubular propulsion units, and the magic strapped on his back, and vertically centered on his spine.

The back unit was special. Just developed, it was being Alpha-tested by Micmac.

The ship's captain, now devoid of the two, off-the-books CIA assets, happened to peer down from the bridge.

"Holy shit!" he gasped.

"I hope you said ship," the First Mate responded.

The captain caught his breath.

"Two men!"

"Yes?"

"On the fo'c'sle!"

He pointed.

• • •

Exiting the harbor, the Mediterranean turned to a full-blown chop.

The zodiac inflatable seemed to leap from one wave to the next.

One of its passengers looked behind over the stern, and noticed a black-coated human form dangling over the rail on the ship's starboard bow.

An order was shouted. "Take him out!"

A gunman fired.

A standard military three-round burst.

Just as Micmac let go of the rail.

He plunged.

Above, the rounds ricocheted.

Off the weighed anchor.

Harmlessly.

Micmac hit the water with propulsion maxed.

Better for the mission he not be run over by the ship.

Never before so encumbered by accoutrements in his UDT and SEAL team days, he settled down, comforted by the stability of their thoughtfully designed devices. Designed to work well separately, or in concert.

The zodiac separated from the pursuing cruise ship at a good clip. Still, Micmac gained.

Just a few clicks from the enemy craft, he received a pop-up visual on his goggles.

Cartagena was in sight.

Time to act.

"Mag? Micmac. Need a decision."

Now alone on the foc's'l rail, Crayle turned to a disturbance behind.

Five men and two women came charging toward him.

Armed.

"Now!"

Micmac struggled to the surface.

Pointed at the zodiac.

Then, one last comm from Crayle.

"And don't forget to duck!"

The former sailor ducked his head.

The missile strapped to his back launched.

Just as the seven ship security officers made it to Crayle.

One of the women, strong as the proverbial ape, pinned his arms as the other cuffed him.

"No testosterone, no problem," Crayle quipped.

Then,

"Five … four … three … two …"

The enemies in the zodiac dove overboard.

All except their leader.

"One …"

Boom!

The missile vaporized the zodiac.

And the leader.

The rest? They swam to shore.

• • •

Micmac caught his breath.

Then, he removed and stuffed his equipment and wetsuit into the bag provided.

He pushed a button. The collection sank to the bottom—to be retrieved later.

As the ship pulled by on Micmac's port side, he waved frantically.

And shouted.

"*Man overboard!*"

Indeed.

CHAPTER 32

Alona met Lenny at the Dawson City airport. There'd been a break in her current case, and her client appeared to be able to stay out of trouble for at least a week. She missed him, and worried about him, and seized the opportunity.

They trouped to a hotel and dropped off their luggage. As a reward, he took her out to one of the favorite haunts as far as nightclubs were concerned. Lenny finished another night at Gertie's. He'd still be there if Alona hadn't hustled him back to the hotel.

Next day, they awoke to the alarm clock blasting *Takin' Care Of Business.*

Lenny hurled a pillow, knocking the clock to the floor and terminating the gross disturbance.

"There. I took care of business," he declared.

"Yes. And there'll be an $800 clock radio on our bill at checkout."

"I'll tell 'em at the front desk it was broke when we got to the room."

"You mean when we entered the room the maid was just finishing … while she listened to it?"

"Hmmm."

"C'mon. Shower, dress, and off to our excursion to the North."

"Oh, yeah. To see the lights."

• • •

They were ready and out in thirty minutes. A short ride to the river, and then onto what resembled a large canoe.

"Good morning, Mr. and Mrs. Lipschitz," said the guide. "I'm Vicki from Vancouver. We need to get going. Environmental considerations will have us paddling, not motoring. Thirty kilometers should have you both in great shape when we're done."

"Eighteen miles?" Alona grimaced. "Thirty-six there and back?"

"Not to worry. The river flows North from Dawson and, coming back, we can cheat on the motor thing. We do this all the time. What could go wrong?"

The couple knew from their spy experiences never to ask that question. Rhetorical or otherwise.

The guide had been right. They cruised at moderate speed and with moderate effort, Northward, toward the Arctic Ocean. In a few hours, their guide told them to stop rowing. She shagged a submerged tree limb and dropped a line over it.

They sat motionless, partaking of a lunch of salmon sandwiches, Kosher pickles, and cold macaroni salad. A six pack of Molson Canadian beer provided liquid refreshment.

It wasn't long before the green neon curtains known as the Northern Lights embedded themselves in the heavens. Something that unique didn't evoke natural grandeur like the rest of the Americas northwest territories, but was, instead, other worldly.

Lenny began to applaud. Slowly, at first. Then with a fervor.

"Mr. Lipschitz, please stop! You'll attract the bears!"

"All the way from Chicago?"

"These bears don't play football. They eat people."

"Oh." He shoved his hands between his thighs to keep them warm.

"Y'know, we could pretend things got exciting."

"So scared we dropped our paddles overboard."

"And then …"

"Well, here we are …"

"Up a creek …"

"Without a paddle."

They turned to their guide, who said, "You won't believe the name of this creek. Think excrement. Spelled S-c-h-i-t-t-apostrophe-s."

She looked at her Apple watch. "Oh, it's time for me to get Alona headed back home. One of her wonderful defense attorney clients needs her. You'll be fine, Lenny. Just head down river … you'll be met … and taken care of. I promise."

Lenny produced a world-class blank look. Headed toward the Artic Ocean with nothing but a canoe and a promise.

The guide pointed out the less environmental means of mobility for the canoe, just as a chopper swooped in and had she and Alona out of Schitt's Creek and headed South on the river. Back toward Dawson.

Lenny was on his own now.

• • •

The Yukon River flowed North with a vengeance this time of year. Regional snow melts gathered forces, supplemental, ensuring the vigorous, turbulent flow.

It might have been a passel of fun had the canoe's lone occupant not been indelibly strapped to the seat.

Some genius had put enough tie wraps together to cross his abdomen, travel rearward along both his sides, then curl under the seat to its forward most aspect where it secured both wrists.

He could still slide sideways, but knew enough to stay perched in the center.

His fingers gripped the board seat at the white knuckle level.

Left, right, and straight ahead he sailed, knowing the fluid would ultimately dump him into the Arctic Ocean.

Time was running out. There. Up ahead. Land's end. Waves crashing ashore. The whole bit.

He'd miss her.

With his entire heart.

Lenny choked back a sob.

Alona had taken a lifelong chance with him. She'd brought a great deal to the party, including the occasional, requisite rebuke.

Just then, a figure appeared ahead on the rocks.

Tall.

Muscular.

Lenny and his canoe closed.

"My God!" he exclaimed. "It's him!"

It wasn't the Creator there for the PI's final reckoning.

Although headed North, Lenny's circumstance was headed South.

The man on the rocks pointed a gun directly at him.

Just seconds to live.

The gun fired.

A booming sound.

Out from the large circumference barrel flew a wad of something.

Lenny would have ducked if his jaw wasn't seriously pressing his collar bone.

A net evolved from the wad of ropes as it flew.

By some miracle, it snagged the front of the canoe.

Previously anchored to the rocks, the vessel now swung away.

It was the travel agent extraordinaire. Darryl.

Lenny's newfound friend stepped forward, extending a hand.

"Lenny, my boy! How the hell are you!"

CHAPTER 33

There they were. The mouth of the Mackenzie River. Staring at the Arctic Ocean. Even in the late Spring, the heavy chill made itself felt.

"The nearest airport is that way." The CIA's go-to, off-the-books travel agent, Darryl, pointed Southeast. "About one hundred klicks as you Yanks like to say. Maybe seventy miles."

"We Yankee civilians say kilometers. It's the military ones who say klicks. It's succinct, Micmac would say. One syllable instead of four."

"With that knowledge—and about 10 bucks Canadian—I can get a Grande Coffee at one of your Starbucks."

"You might have to travel a bit for that."

"Speaking of which, the rest of your Darryl-guided tour will take us over the top."

He pointed left to a beached canoe, approximately half again the size of their current one. "That's our ride."

Lenny peered at the watercraft that appeared brand new with an oar poking out each side, and a hefty motor hanging over the stern transom.

The idea of setting out in that boat West over the top of Alaska didn't click right away.

Darryl anticipated the reaction. "It's okay, Scrub. Your favorite travel guide has it all planned. We'll catch lunch at Prudhoe Bay, then dinner at Barrow. We'll stop for the night. Tomorrow, through the Bering Sea."

"Let me get this right. Thousands of kilometers in a canoe? In the Arctic Ocean?"

"It's okay, Scrub. The First Nations did it all the time. You see, the currents head that way this time of year." Darryl laughed his substantive trademark laugh.

Darryl stood and opened the large duffel he'd been sitting on. He handed Lenny what appeared to be a flight suit.

"We just plug them in … and stay warm."

They motored over to the new craft and transferred their meager belongings.

Lenny surveyed the situation. The word insane seemed to pop up frequently in his thoughts. "Okay, we each take an oar—one on each side—and have the motor going. That makes it a hybrid. Politically correct."

"I hadn't thought of that, Scrub. But … whatever floats your boat."

They both laughed at that one. Then, they pushed off into the sea of the Great North.

CHAPTER 34

On the flight East, Miao-Yin had apprized Hekka and Phoebe on what the remote piece of territory known as the Chukchi Peninsula had for its history.

"Where we're heading is the Easternmost peninsula of Asia. The end closest to Alaska is Cape Dezhnev. And there, the village called Uelen. There is Russian military there. They receive little governance from Moscow—I mean Saint Petersburg—so we must be careful around the Russians."

Hekka indulged her curiosity. "Any non-military Russians?" She didn't know that a Russian general had flown by helicopter out to Big Diomede Island, and lost his life a few years back. All while her husband, Magus, was busy saving President-to-be Kimbel Stones' life.

"There are a few. Left over from the Soviet days. The communists would grab people, and sentence them to work the Siberian mines. The Convict Economy, it was called. Gold, lead, tin, zinc, et cetera. Most residents are indigenous, which is your research interest.

"The Chukchi consists of rolling flat lands bounded on the West by the Chukotka Mountains, and by the Pacific Ocean on the East. We have the Chukchi Sea on the North, and the Bering Sea South. By the way, the Eastern waters are called the Bering Straight. It's about 60 kilometers—37 miles—over to the Seward Peninsula of West Alaska."

"So my ancestors needed to sail across one of the most dramatic seas on Earth to introduce themselves to the wild and wooly West … of North America."

"Scientists believe that long ago the Chukchi Peninsula was physically connected to what is now Alaska. Alaska was simply Eastern Siberia."

"So America bought that, and renamed it Alaska?"

"Yes."

"What did my ancestors do for sustenance?

"They hunted. They trapped. Some herded reindeer. They slaughtered some and then cooked the meat. Except, of course, right before Christmas."

They chuckled over that one.

"About halfway across the water are the Diomede Islands. One big, one small."

"Then in the worst case, those peoples of long ago only needed to cross about twenty miles to the islands, and another twenty to North America."

"You are very mathematical, Hekka."

"You are very generous. Let's say, arithmetical."

Another chuckle.

"I know about the geography now, but how about the people? What is it that links them to my tribe, the Serrano?"

"Recent research concluded that the Chukchi are the closest peoples of Asia to the American indigenous peoples, like your Serrano."

"Hmmm. What about religion?"

"The religion was and is spirit-oriented. All have a spirit inside."

"Wow. That's quite similar to ours."

"Religion would survive the transition from Asia to your lands, wouldn't it? Even over thousands of years."

"You're right."

"I almost forgot. The language. It is complex, and it appears to be linked to that of the Eskimo. I haven't found a meaningful investigation into that, though."

"Well, a new found PhD needs to have something to do."

"Other than spying?"

"Yes. Other than spying."

The intercom interrupted.

"This is Marli. Hope you had a good flight. Buckle up. Down in fifteen."

• • •

They landed at the Uelen airport, one overseen by the Russian military.

Their guide hopped out first, showing the officer-in-charge documents bearing Czarina Anastasia Romanova's seal. The officer waved okay.

Hekka and Phoebe trouped off the Dassault Falcon unmolested. Their pilot and co-pilot unloaded their suitcases, then turned their attention to refueling the team jet.

A local guide, who spoke Chukchi, Russian, and excellent English, met them, loading everyone and everything onto what appeared to be a weathered and aged yellow American school bus.

"Apparently the snow cat is in the shop," Phoebe quipped.

The vehicle trundled off to what appeared to be a large, ancient hut.

"Oh," said the guide. "This is our indigenous museum. We're next door. For lunch. They serve the food the originals ate. Or similar."

• • •

Inside, they sat at what Westerners would call picnic tables.

The guide passed out menus in the three relevant languages.

Hekka took a look.

"Let's see if the food is similar to the Serrano."

Phoebe checked it out. She nodded what appeared to convey her approval.

"This first one sounds good. Actually, they all do. Hard to choose."

"Hmmm," Hekka replied. "*Vilmulimul.* Reindeer. Stomach. Oh, and chocked full of reindeer hooves, livers, ears, kidneys … and blood."

"Wonder if I can get that to go." Phoebe smirked.

"Here's one where they bury sea mammal meat, dig it up, and eat it after six months or so."

"Yeah. It's hard to choose."

She turned.

"Hey, guide? Do you have a McDonalds?"

They all settled on the boiled reindeer meat with bone marrow topping.

Yum.

• • •

After the meal, they ambled next door to the museum, devoid of any take-home delicacies.

A short browse, and Hekka found what she needed.

A quiver of arrows with white feathers.

Just like those she'd found in Central Asia on her previous research trip.

CHAPTER 35

Hekka's Chukchi cohort drove them to Cape Dezhnev, not far from Uelen. She remembered President Stones' tale of the town. A Russian general had flown to Big Diomede Island in the Bering Straight during President Stones' sojourn as an NSA field operative and intel gatherer so long ago.

"Mrs. Crayle, these boats were used to transfer your ancestors across to the Seward Peninsula, some 37 miles distant. In today's Alaska."

"They are covered in animal skins. That construction technique survived all the way down to my Big Bear homeland in the Southern California mountains."

"There's something else."

The Chukchi pulled out a hard-sided satchel and opened it. "This is yours to keep. A few keepsakes to remember me by."

Hekka went immediately to the glass tube. A white feather.

"Oh, that. Probably insignificant," he said. "An ancient arrow feather. I heard the indigenous tribes of North America used bows and arrows to hunt. Any truth to that?"

Hekka drew a pouch from her purse and produced the white arrow feather she'd received in Central Asia.

She'd discovered the link. From there to the Chukchi Peninsula and across to Alaska. And South.

Game—Set—Match!

She'd now traced her ancestors' migrations from India to America.

She had her proof.

She tucked away her treasures, then helped tote the craft to the water's edge.

The Bering Straight she'd seen on TV, with the crab fishermen working in extreme winds and seas, stood right there before her.

And it howled.

CHAPTER 36

First, they'd spent a week crossing the Atlantic, with stops at the Portuguese Madeira Island, two stops each in Morocco and Spain, and now on to Rome with a much welcomed 'at sea' day interposed.

Magus Crayle, Director of Central Intelligence, at least by title, felt the need to force the President Stones' requisite relaxation in order to set up his future life for success. That meant no more brain messing sessions with Doctor Rorschach.

"The two of you may discuss anything here," said the ship's spa director, Kelly.

"I'm not sure the two of you are cleared … for everything."

"We both have sufficient clearance. I can get the president on the line …"

Kelly held the CIA Smartphone aloft.

"For me to relax, I need everyone else to relax. So, no Kimbel."

"Kimbel?" Kelly smiled. "First names, are we?"

"One thing I've noticed about spies. The ones that stay alive. They never miss out on insights."

“And how insightful are you?” she asked rhetorically.

He turned to Micmac, who was undergoing Tracy’s initial massage prep.

“Here’s a little recent memory dump. Before the first time we visited Madeira and I held the first Summit Meeting, about a year ago, I set up the blackmailing of the world’s three top clergy members. The Pope, the Grand Ayatollah, and the Chief Rabbi of Judaism. Remember?”

“I was the one who frisked them,” Micmac replied. “Just outside the private and bug-swept room.”

“That’s why they weren’t smiling when they came in. Now, if Phoebe had done it …”

“You are channeling Lenny again.”

“I find channeling Lenny relaxing. Phoebe thinks your wife does, too.”

“Phoebe would relax … right after putting the little P.I. out of her misery.”

Crayle went on.

“Summit B, the second one, did—we did—in Casablanca. The final one, Summit C, was Jerusalem. The perfect venue.”

“Well, we’ve hit the first two venues on this cruise. Hmmm. Coincidence?”

“Yes. Coincidence.”

The ladies started rubbing in expert fashion back and neck muscles.

“Oh. That feels good,” the men chorused.

Five minutes later, they were both fast asleep.

• • •

Once they revived, they did normal, relaxing activities aboard their cruise ship.

They ate.

They ate.

And they ate some more.

For a brief intermission, they went out to the main pool. There, Crayle relaxed in a lounge chair under a more-than-sufficient coating of Number 50 tanning oil.

Micmac amazed onlookers by casually swimming 50 laps of the large pool.

• • •

The next day, the two were up, bleary eyed, just as the ship pulled into Italy's Civitavecchia Harbor.

They were ready to go as the gangway was fastened into place.

Ashore, they met their guide, who drove them the harrowing miles into Rome proper.

First stop: The Hard Rock Café.

This visit, there was no espionage or other 'out there' behaviors exhibited.

To their surprise, a band took the stage. A band they recognized.

The British MI-6 spy group.

The Apostles.

Crayle and Micmac tossed waves at Matthew, Mark, Luke, and Jane. They waved back.

Being in the city that hosted one of the world's top religions, the Apostles played all the songs in their Hard Rock playlist, and even let Micmac sit in on one.

Highway To Hell, by the Aussie group, AC/DC.

After, the two relaxing spies finished their substantial meals, and their waiter boxed up the remains.

• • •

Back at the ship, Micmac started to place the leftovers into the smallish, stateroom refrigerator.

He popped the cardboard box open just to check on the contents. Were these their leftovers?

"Hey, Mag. Check this out."

He lifted the contents.

A small, wood and metal treasure chest. Locked tight.

"Number four."

"I wonder how many are in a set."

He shrugged. "Oh, well. I'll put it in the backpack with the others."

CHAPTER 37

The two American spies, on their U.S. President Stones-prescribed relaxation cruise, hard partied the night away at Rome's Hard Rock Café, at least until 3 P.M. Their ship had threatened in its Daily Patter publication to be *All Aboard* and underway by 5 P.M.

Having imbibed a little too much alcohol, which can happen at the Hard Rock, they opened the windows of their transport vehicle and sent one-fingered salutes to the American Embassy.

They had many times put their lives on the line for their country, and were just having a little fun. Both knew that this particular embassy was a test bed for the latest technologies.

They were well aware the facility's ultra-resolution surveillance cameras and AI facial recognition software would have ID'd them instantly, and the images would be in Kimbel Stones' hands forthwith.

They hoped he'd get the joke, shake his head, and even laugh for once. The man was just too serious.

And they were really relaxed.

Back on the Island Princess, the pair elevatored up to the top deck.

There'd be a *Sail Away Party*.

With umbrella drinks.

All of that came to pass and, finally, they made it to their staterooms to hit their racks.

They were exhausted.

Dinner would have to wait for another day.

• • •

They rose bright and early the next day, and set off to their spa sessions.

Kelly and Tracy noticed the bloodshot eyes.

"Party last night, did we?"

Crayle responded first. "Keeping up with a sailor is hard work."

Micmac shrugged. "You did well. The whole thing was like a liberty call. From the old days." He glanced over at the ladies. "The two of you should come along next time. In Messina. Or when we get to Greece."

"Oh, Tracy and I are tea-totalers. Not much fun."

Tracy burst out laughing.

"Y'know, Mag. Lenny's sense of humor keeps popping up. I wonder how he's doing."

"Don't know. This being dark on comms outside of an op is a nuisance. He has lame jokes pop into his head frequently. I'd be surprised if we're not at war with Canada by now."

"Yeah. And your spouse. It would be great to know how all that indigenous research of hers over in Asia is coming along."

"Well, we'll be finished up in a few days when we dock in Cypress, and heading home. I suspect she'll already be back."

The ship's captain interrupted their thoughts via a ceiling-mounted speaker. He advised that the ship was formally docked, under shore power, and ready to allow passengers ashore.

Off they went.

• • •

Within twenty minutes, they walked down the pier, with no spy guide attending this time.

Crayle took the opportunity to exercise his memory. Ole Doc Rorschach and the president would like that.

"Here we are. Ambulating down Via Garibaldi in Messina, Sicily. A main drag. You can verify my memories since you've been here before … in combat mode."

"Spy combat, Mag. Black ops. Not quite as overt as normal combat."

Crayle smirked.

"Continuing … sitting here on Messina Strait, just across from the Italian peninsula, this location was strategic. Many conquerors. The Spanish even ran the place for awhile. "It was founded by the Greeks. If I remember. The 8th century BC."

They stopped at the cathedral square. Plenty of room out front for worshippers and, yes, tourists to assemble.

They'd observe the tall clock tower, physically separate from the main religious structure. And focus their attention on the moving figures and giant clock.

"The bell tower has one of the largest astronomical clocks in the world, Micmac. The animated statues add to its grandeur. They display religious and other history at noon."

Micmac checked his CIA Smartwatch.

"Right … about … now!"

The bells chimed their tune, while the figures moved as if in time to the music.

"What else do you remember about this place?"

"After a number of conquests and occupations of the city, the Arabs took over. Remember? They did that on the Spain and Portugal peninsula."

"Yeah. Speaking of them, I wonder what our friends in the New Persia are up to. That Ayatollah guy always seems to be up to something."

"Well, the far out there portion of his religion believes they get a free, express trip to Paradise if they die fighting the good fight."

"And The Good Fight is determined by folks such as our Grand Ayatollah Jahni."

"Just so. I wonder what our old friend, Jahni, is up to."

Miles to the Southeast, that musing was being answered.

CHAPTER 38

Crayle was up at the crack of dawn. Micmac remained in La La Land, not having had to be up at reveille for a number of years.

In stealth mode, Crayle unlatched and opened the sliding door, and stepped out onto the balcony, closing the door behind.

There it was. The cruise port town of Katakolon, Greece, lay dead ahead. Shaped like a left parenthesis open end toward the sea, the town of just over 500 residents seemed to welcome the cruise ship into its grasp. It seemed much too calm to be a spider to the fly sort of welcome, so Crayle took a moment to relax his *en garde* nature, and enjoy the spectacle. Especially after Madeira. And Morocco and Italy.

The air felt fresh and clean, but the aroma, he swore, hinted of olives.

Within the hour, he shaved, showered, dressed, and headed out to the gangway. Devoid of armaments, he passed security scrutiny without so much as a notice. Barely off the stairs, he noticed a man maybe 5'8" with dark, wavy hair swept back into a junior mullet accompanied by a woman with short black hair and a couple of inches shorter. The man spoke.

"Uh, Mr. Smith, I presume."

A couple of verbal handshakes later, Crayle-Smith responded. "I'm here for the Olympia excursion." He reached his hand to the man. "Costas?" Then, the woman. "Dina?"

Both of the Greeks shook their heads, and chorused "No" to complete the pre-arranged, two-stage, spy handshake process.

A short walk down the pier, they entered a non-characteristic Audi sedan, and set off for the famed first site of the eponymous Olympic games.

Dina had gone off with Micmac in tow. Costas drove Crayle past the museum to the original Olympic field. At precisely 100 meters, he stopped, turned, scanned the air, then down.

Crayle, in his characteristic New Balance tennis shoes, took off at moderate speed as Costas recorded, or pretended to record, the event.

Halfway along, puffs of dirt began to spring up in front and to the sides. No sounds. Just dirt.

Crayle was a quick study. He'd seen bullets hitting dirt before.

He took off at full speed, looking for cover.

There was none.

His head spun to the right toward a bunch of bushes. He saw a flash of light. A riflescope.

That the shooter didn't taken him out with the first shot registered that he was either being warned, or the shooter was a sadist.

Crayle waved arms and hands franticly at Costas, who smiled and waved back.

At 80 meters, Crayle threw a quick glance back to his right. The silenced gunshots had stopped abruptly.

There Dina stood next to the bushes with what appeared to be a suppressed, James Bond-style Walther PPK, blowing real smoke off its tip.

Just as he ran past his Greek spy guide, Crayle veered right, running toward the bushes. He arrived breathless at Dina's side.

"We received a heads up just five minutes ago." She peered down at the partially hidden, lifeless body and his assault-style long gun.

"Thanks. I'd say it in Greek if I could."

Two men, looking like a threat, walked toward them. One pushed a wheelbarrow. Unceremoniously, the two piled the gunman into the barrow, covered him with a man-sized tarp, and were off.

"Let's get back to Costas, fill him in, and exit stage left in case that guy had friends."

Together, they turned toward the field. Costas was nowhere to be seen.

In the distance, a man loaded what looked like a limp body into a helicopter, and it lifted off.

The two ran in that direction, knowing it was in vain. They arrived to see the chopper just cruise out of sight. Dina leaned down and picked up a piece of paper. The writing on it was in Greek. She read it aloud, sounding rather gloomy.

"I know where they're going."

She looked up to see the quizzical look on Crayle's face.

She translated as she re-read the note.

"All roads lead to Rhodes. After Crete."

• • •

Having arrived next in the port city, Hania, on the Greek island of Crete, their new guide, Elantra, took them directly to the top-rated restaurant, *Portes*.

"It's the best place in town for creative Cretan, not Cretin, cooking." She spelled out the a-n and the i-n.

"We certainly don't want to run into any cretins on our relaxation voyage."

Micmac checked out the menu.

"Hmmm. I think I'll pass on the wild snails. I'll have the marinated little fish. The *gavros.*"

He glanced over at Crayle.

"For me, it's the stuffed fish baked in paper, it says."

The waiter nodded that he understood the order, given in English. "And to drink?"

"Pick out something. A Cretan wine. Your best."

The waiter left.

"Your best?" Micmac shrugged.

"Remember. Uncle Kimbel, President of all the United States, leader of the free world, is picking up the tab."

• • •

The wine came in short order. The two men toasted their rich uncle, Kimbel Stones.

Then, the delicious repast, and, before they could get out the door, "Your leftovers, Sirs."

Crayle took the bag.

• • •

Back aboard the ship, they checked their latest bag of leftovers.

Another wood and metal treasure chest.

Number five.

And still with the impregnable lock.

"Oh, well," the two chorused.

CHAPTER 39

It was yet another day aboard the Island Princess.

Crayle and sidekick Micmac finished their new morning ritual at the spa, then debarked the ship.

On the pier, they encountered Kelly and Tracy, whom they'd seen a mere ten minutes before in the spa.

"Surprise," Kelly exclaimed. "We're your guides for today. You'll have to get used to our unaccented English."

"You're getting the day off?"

"Sort of. Like I said, we're your guides today. We are taking you to a museum."

"We aren't that old."

"It's special."

"And relaxing," Tracy added.

The two women led their charges to a van only with tinted windows around the cab. With privacy in back.

Opening the side door and leaning in, Kelly flipped open a container along the passenger side. She withdrew a pair of semi-automatic handguns plus four spare clips. Fully-loaded clips.

They arrived at the outskirts of Rhodes Island's eponymous capitol in a mere fifteen minutes, and they came to a stop in a deserted alley.

Someone outside slid open the passenger-side door.

Crayle was surprised.

"Dina!"

"Good morning, gentlemen. And thank you for coming."

"Let's see. Two guns. And ammo. My mind reading app is in the shop. Care to explain?"

She smiled. "I traced the kidnapping of my Costas to this place. Remember? They took him at Olympia?"

"I remember. Did you clear this little black op with President Stones?"

"Of course. He said you could relax when it's over."

"So, if we survive the extraction of Costas, and make it to our final cruise stop in Cypress, we can relax."

"Just so … come."

Dina marched the four out of the alley and down the street to a museum-quality building. She stepped past a *Closed For Maintenance* sign just outside the front door.

She tried the knob. The door was locked.

Micmac came forward, and retrieved a small device from his sport coat's inner pocket. He attached it to the knob, and touched an app icon on his Smartphone.

The device activated with barely a sound. Not even a click as the door opened an inch.

The four followed Dina inside.

The room was big. There were tall glass cases around its periphery.

The only sign of life sat tied to a chair at the room's center.

Costas. Bound and gagged.

The five of them were by now locked and loaded. All armed and ready for what came next.

Five men appeared, apparently from nowhere.

All were armed and sported short blond hair.

The impromptu spy team dove behind ancient artifacts.

And the fun began.

The five Aryans had for some reason armed themselves with German World War I relic revolvers. And ammo.

The guns either failed to operate, or when they were able to drop the hammer, the ancient cartridges refused to fire.

All but one of them went down in five seconds.

The final one, as if on drugs, charged. In the next instant, the cover the team had chosen would be of no use.

Quick, Costas pushed his weight to his right.

Then slung it left.

He and his chair toppled in that direction.

Right in the Aryan's path.

The gunman tripped over the new obstruction, and crashed to the floor.

An easy target, the final enemy was neutralized in short order.

Quickly, Dina, Kelly, and Tracy converged on Costas, freed him, and removed the gag.

"Thank you for rescuing me," were his first words. "The food here is lousy."

Crayle and Micmac laughed the loudest. It seemed Lenny's sense of humor had definitely gone international.

"Oh, they left this on my lap."

Costas handed Dina a bag.

She reached in, then handed the contents to Crayle.

Another wood and metal treasure chest.

Number six.

• • •

On the way back to the ship, Crayle took the opportunity to do a little remembering exercise. Of someone the team knew well. From a while back.

• • •

His birth in the French Southwest had not been a notable birth. Born to work-a-day parents, he arrived as just another French baby of the male persuasion. He grew up attending local schools, doing fairly well in grades, giving his parents high hopes for a stint with the prestigious *École des Haute Études Commerciales* on Boulevard Mortier in Paris.

And that's the way it went down. But, on graduation day, tragedy struck. Not familiar with France's premier city, his parents passed through the arrondisement just as Middle Eastern terrorists struck. The target appeared to be the stock market, but the perpetrators were off by a couple of districts.

He graduated, not able to pick out his parents in the celebratory throng.

As valedictorian, he'd been announced, not by his common given name, but as the future King of France. Since the monarchy had passed away long before, that wasn't likely. But Charles the King, Charleroi, still sounded good. And it stuck.

He decided his career would possess an international nature. For that, he would require a fluency and a cultural affinity in the commercial language of the world, English.

He took to the Internet to research the prospects. It seemed the world did not want English with an English accent. Or Scottish. Or Welsh. Or Irish. It wanted an American lilt.

Off he went to graduate school. In Bangor, Maine. What a mistake. It wasn't clear from his year there that the Maine-iacs, as he termed them, could even understand each other. That offered the rest of the English-speaking world little hope. Second year, he transferred to the University of North Carolina in Charlotte. Mistake number two.

Third year found him in the bastion of accent free American. Southern California. With some funds from the French government, and a substantial insurance payoff from his parents' policy, he set up shop in Del Mar, California. A bachelor pad with an ocean view.

The University of California, San Diego, as an English major resulted in him finally being on the right path. He needed an elective, he was informed, and went for the one class that intrigued him. Espionage 101.

When he finished his coursework with honors, he felt he'd repaid his parents for giving him his life. Their son would be a success.

While there, he developed a relationship with a girl whose hobby was watching old detective shows on TV. One in particular caught Charleroi's eye. Agatha Christie. And her premier character, Hercule Poirot. Though the shows were presented in the English language, the Frenchness of Poirot provided a special grounding. Charleroi started work on a bushy, ends-curled-up moustache. He mimicked Poirot at every turn. French-accented English was a natural.

Back in France with his master's degree, he wasn't sure where to go next. Then, it hit him. Because his parents were taken from him by terrorists, he applied for, and was accepted into, the Direction Générale de Securité Extérieure. The General Directorate for External Security. The vaunted DGSE. Headquartered on Boulevard Mortier. Paris.

And so concluded Crayle's memory. Of Charleroi. The French spy.

CHAPTER 40

The heavens wore dark, and were still.

Crayle posited himself on a lounge chair. The absence of sound from the adjoining stateroom or its balcony implied that his associate and friend, Micmac, was still in the sack—as the former sailor would say.

Glancing to his left toward the ship's bow provided the only view, other than of seawater, available.

A worthy sight.

Off to the horizon, a plethora of lights shone bright. They highlighted the port city's two tall buildings.

As the ship approached today's first destination, suddenly, a body took shape as it skirted the stateroom-to-rail partition that separated the balconies.

Micmac.

"You might want to put on some clothes, shipmate."

The former sailor glanced downward.

"Oh. Uh, Phoebe and I sleep naked. You know, like the jaybirds do."

"T.M.I., Micmac."

"No problem. I'll get fixed up before we're close enough to port that anyone'll notice."

"You mean like the two women one deck up and a bit towards the stern? The ones that are waving?"

Micmac thought it was a joke, but looked up anyway.

"Oh!"

He waved back.

Then, he plopped onto the other lounge chair.

"Ah, I'm relaxed," he said. "How about you? This whole cruise thing was for your recovery. Through relaxation."

"Let's see. Madeira, Morocco, Spain, Italy, Greece? Other than deadly encounters and a constantly precocious mindset, I think I'm good. And those treatments in the spa added relax on top of relax."

"Yeah. Kelly and Tracy. We'll need to tip well."

"You bet."

In seconds, they were both asleep.

• • •

Next they knew, the captain was tooting the smokestack whistle, announcing their entry into Limassol Harbor in the island country, Cypress.

"Quick, Micmac. In through my stateroom. Through the shared door. Get something on. Before you become the hit of the capitol city."

"I'm a sailor. I don't become a hit 'til I go ashore."

"We're on vacation, but we're still spies. Number one rule: *Don't get noticed.*"

"Oh, Mag? I almost forgot. I arranged for spa treatments. Before we make port! Gotta hurry!"

• • •

They did.

They arrived at the spa twenty minutes later.

Kelly and Tracy had no other clients this early.

They led the two men to a special room, placed a *Closed for Maintenance* sign on the door, closed it, and locked it.

Kelly, dressed entirely in black, spoke.

"We have something special for you gentlemen."

"Marital exit visas," Micmac quipped.

"Uh, no. What we have is from the mother ship. From Langley."

Tracy handed Crayle a small wood and metal box. Same dimensions as the previous six.

"What's this all about, Kelly? The little boxes? I feel like, on this trip, we're always the last to know."

At that point, Micmac removed his backpack, opened it, and produced the aforementioned six treasure chests.

"Now there are seven."

"Notice anything?"

Crayle glanced at Tracy, then Kelly, then looked down.

"They are all the same. Except the last one Tracy just provided has gold metal hardware, instead of silver like the others."

"Gold means this little Langley antic is over." Kelly turned to her colleague.

"Tracy?"

Tracy produced a strange looking key. And handed it to Crayle.

"Open up, Mr. Crayle."

"I'll have my technical man do the honors."

Micmac took the key, and opened the boxes. Carefully. No telling what might pop out.

Both men leaned over the treasure chests.

"What the hell! They're … they're Scrabble tiles!"

Kelly smiled. "Tracy, the SIM card?"

"This is special CIA issue. Works only with Company Smartphones."

Crayle installed the card.

"Touch the US app," Kelly instructed.

"As in *us*? Or United States?"

"Un-Scrabble. You photograph the seven tiles. The app un-Scrabbles them."

"There may be some re-arranging to do at The Company when I get back. Spending their time on this sort of thing."

"Oh, c'mon. We're having fun. It's part of your relaxation regimen."

Crayle took a deep breath, and released it. Then, he checked his phone.

"It's realigning them."

He reached down, and placed the actual tiles in 'app' order.

"There. D-I-O-M-E-D-E."

Tracy closed the boxes, and turned them over.

Pressed into the wood, each one had another letter.

Crayle took a photo. And checked the app.

"P-R-O-C-E-E-D."

Kelly folded her arms giving the visual impression of a teacher about to instruct her students.

"You will proceed into town. Stay out of trouble. Be at the Limassol International Airport by noon. The pilot, a Brazilian asset named Flori, will take you East."

"Take us to Diomede? Which one? There are two."

"The one big enough to have an airstrip."

"We'll need to get our baggage, then."

"Not so. Tracy and I will see that your baggage, including your sidearms and ammunition, arrive intact and on time at the jet."

Tracy interrupted.

"This just in. You need to make a brief stop on the way."

"Of course. For fuel."

"Uh, no. In Jerusalem."

• • •

It was dark when they awoke from the sedation. The world's three top clerics found themselves in a dark, dank room. The only light seeped in through a partially open doorway.

Rabbi Kushner led them out and up a set of stairs. At the next level up, three jaws dropped at the splendor. The floor was bounded by a circular structure that appeared to rise a couple of stories, culminating in the inside aspect of a large dome.

"The Dome of the Rock," muttered the Muslim.

It truly was.

The Rabbi and the Pope stepped to a two-foot-high fence that surrounded the famous rock.

The stone was basically flat, but it displayed texture and curves befitting its many millennia of weathering before the outside structure was built.

The Grand Ayatollah of the new Persia announced what all of them knew. "Mohammed stood at the rock's center, and rose to the heavens."

As dawn broke, the darkness evolved to light.

There, at the stone's center, stood a too familiar figure.

The American.

Mag Crayle.

"This is the day. It is your day. It is our day. It's the world's day."

Before him, they observed an ornate gold box. Shaped like a coffin, its gold structure undoubtedly real.

The Pope reached out to touch it, but felt a restraining hand on his forearm. The Rabbi's hand. He stopped.

The Ayatollah stepped around them as Crayle flipped the side latches open, and lifted the lid.

The Muslim cleric reached out and touched the contents.

A single tree branch.

An olive branch.

A universal symbol of peace.

He felt a hand as it touched his. Then, a third.

There they stood. Hand on top of hand. With an olive branch.

Although none of them expected America's new CIA Director to levitate up to heaven, the magnitude of what he had just done captured their souls.

Grand Ayatollah Jahni glanced at the other three.

And spoke.

"Peace."

CHAPTER 41

Crayle and Micmac made it back to Israel's primary international airport.

As reliable as the sunrise and the sunset, Flori had the Dassault Falcon business and spy jet refueled and ready to go.

For the first time the two spies felt they had some sort of certainty regarding their future. They were going to Diomede. The big one of the two. Abandoned by the Russians long ago.

Crayle shook his head, sporting a Hekka-like minimalist smile.

"All we have to do is successfully fly through the air spaces of Jordan, Iraq, Iran—"

"Make that Persia. Then, dot-dot-dot. Then Mongolia. Much of Siberia. Finally, to Diomede Island in the Bering Straight."

"The dot-dot-dot?"

"It's called an ellipsis. For the several Central Asia countries. Like Kazakhstan."

"As long as none of them shoot at us. And flying over the East half of Siberia, shoot, we just might overfly Hekka and Phoebe. We can wave."

"We'll have to wave a lot. Won't be able to see them from forty thou."

"We'll be at fifty thousand feet," popped over the intercom.

"Flori? Are you listening in?"

Click.

• • •

The two lasted another half an hour, then went aft and caught some serious shuteye.

All of the President Stones-ordered relaxation had worn them out.

• • •

Hours later, Flori broke the silence.

"Down in fifteen. Two fueling stops accomplished, and we're on final approach for Big Diomede. Buckle up, and hang on. The runway there is really close to being long enough.

• • •

And they were down in fifteen.

No fancy terminal. Just a substantial-sized yurt.

When the baggage had been removed, Crayle asked the operative question.

"What now, Flori?"

"Have the baggage handlers schlep the bags to your rooms."

She pointed toward the circular fortress at the center of the island.

"Baggage handlers? This place is desolate. As I recall, when I rescued a nearly dead Kimbel Stones during a blizzard here, that fort was manned by a bunch of Russian troops—ones who'd royally pissed off someone to get stationed in one of the most desolate places on Earth."

"So," Flori replied. "Who'd you piss off?"

It was worth a chuckle.

"Looks like the baggage boys are on strike, gentlemen. Grab your bags and head on over to the fort. There might be signs inside to get you situated. I understand there's plenty of food and drink, and the heaters work."

"Wait a minute. How much do you know?"

Too late.

Flori had the door closed and buttoned up. Shortly, the jet headed to be positioned for take off.

Then, gone.

• • •

The two men, suitcases in hand, headed to the fortress designed to resemble the Washington, D.C. pentagon's functionality. It had the open, park-like space at its center.

The spa ladies, Kelly and Tracy, were there to greet them.

The Big Diomede fort—the one Kimbel Stones had slipped into a few years ago to grab serious intelligence information prior to his incarnation as American president—resembled a giant cheese wheel, the segments of the fort delineated like pie slices. At the center a circular area contained the main administrative office. It was the most protected against an assault, and the commandant could call in resources from any segment without the others being aware. The pie slices absorbed energy, further protecting the center's occupants. The final touch was a special button. Pressed, it raised the central disc for a view of the rest of the fort and beyond.

CHAPTER 42

After a fitful, uneventful sleep, the only apparent residents of Russia's Big Diomede Island went to a small boat harbor to check it out.

None could imagine anyone sailing or motoring to the Diomedes, but they were not all that far from Eastern Russia or Alaska.

On a perfect day, with a moderate breeze from the West, they unloaded picnic baskets left at Crayle's room at the abandoned fortress, and launched into cold cuts and cheese slices.

A half hour in, something out to sea caught Micmac's eye.

"Hey, everyone! Look!"

He pointed.

What headed directly their way appeared to be a large canoe.

It drew nearer.

Crayle lifted a pair of binoculars that'd been left in his room.

"My God! I can't believe my eyes! It's Hekka!"

Micmac couldn't believe his eyes.

"And Phoebe!"

"They're supposed to be in Siberia!"

"Mag …" Micmac waved his hard to the West. "That over there is Siberia."

The two men jumped up, and waved franticly, and shouted. "Over here!"

It became clear that the two women in the canoe were as surprised as the two men ashore.

Then, Hekka and Phoebe noticed the two attractive ladies, Kelly and Tracy, with their husbands.

Crayle noticed the notice.

"Oh. It's okay. They're spies like us!"

• • •

In the ensuing minutes, the seagoing pair paddled up to the dock, and their husbands lashed the canoe to the cleats provided.

• • •

"What in the world are you doing here, Hekka? You're supposed to be researching. In Siberia." He pointed.

"Over there."

"Great to see you, too. We were exploring the ocean passage to Alaska. The one my ancestors took. For my research?"

Crayle appeared nonplussed.

"This is just too, too much. As if someone planned this whole deal. From the proverbial get-go."

Hekka shook her head.

"Who would have that sort of knowledge? And the will and resources to pull it off?"

Who, indeed.

CHAPTER 43

The drama was far from over. Heads turned, fingers pointed, and a variety of expletives sounded.

Off on the nearby seas, the tops of masts appeared near the horizon.

All watched.

Enraptured.

• • •

Kelly and Tracy positioned themselves behind the four Crayle team members, and got into some serious neck massaging.

"Relax," they said. Repeatedly.

• • •

"From that direction, it is going to take them a while to get here," Crayle told them all. "We'll get lunch at the fort, then check back here in an hour."

• • •

Precisely one hour later, all current residents of Big Diomede reassembled back at the port.

Just in time.

The several boats were reefing their sails. All were both wooden and ancient. The lead boat was the biggest.

As the sailors lashed the sails of the lead boat to its masts, all observed the quite tall man at the bow. He waved and smiled.

The man wore a deep purple and white cloak with gold embellishments.

"Everyone recognize the appliqués?" Crayle glanced around.

"*Fleur-de-Lis.*"

"A country's iconic symbol," Hekka added. She looked back to her husband, and nodded.

"Ladies and gentlemen. I give you Jean-Marc Lalumière. King Louis XX of *La Belle France.*"

• • •

And so it was. The king and elegantly dressed queen of France had just arrived by sailing ship to the little island called Diomede.

With the ship tied up to a dock, and a gangway installed, the pair stepped off and greeted, individually, the people ashore.

Just then, there were two outcries. They came from Tracy and Kelly, who were jumping up and down, pointing out to sea.

At more masts.

Headed their way.

CHAPTER 44

There was a huge commotion among the Big and Little Diomedans gathered along the Southern shore. In the distance was the explanation for all the commotion.

Just their side of the horizon, not one, not two, but five full-sized aircraft carriers and support vessels, headed their way.

The flotilla continued until within range, then helicopters lifted off from their flight decks, formed a single line, and proceeded North.

One by one, they landed. Military exited first. Then, from the fourth, Crayle saw someone he knew well. The man and his small entourage headed straight for him.

"Well, I hope I'm not late," said a smiling President Stones.

"Today we're waving late penalties for heads of state," Crayle opined as he returned the smile. "I see your choppers are all labeled Marine One."

"Security."

"Better to use Marine Two."

"I wish the Vice President no harm."

"No one would risk war with us by taking out the V.P."

"Noted."

"Did you pick the fourth one for your ride?"

"Random number generator, Micmac."

Crayle turned. His one and only former SEAL just shrugged.

The rest of the team shrugged. It seemed they'd all mastered the French version of *I dunno*.

Crayle took the lead.

"Let's all get inside and get warm."

Crayle considered. So, when Micmac headed West for a bit prior to his swim, he'd been in contact with Stones, sensing that is was safe for the president to continue in.

He and the former SEAL would talk later.

CHAPTER 45

It was Stones who'd made all the arrangements. He'd utilized the team's rock steady travel agent, Darryl, to set it all up. He knew from experience there would be nothing left undone.

Big surprises, but no surprises.

The superspy and global strategist led his entourage to Big Diomede Island's East coast docks. There, they waited.

"Look!" Alona, who'd arrived with the president's entourage, pointed.

At first, all followed her extended arm and finger. Across the narrow 2.4 mile—3.8 kilometer—expanse, stood Little Diomede. On the West side of the International Date Line. Yesterday Island.

"No," she yelled. "There!"

They saw it. The top of a ship's mast. With banners flapping in the chill Bering Sea wind.

As it approached, the tops of billowing sails flailed in the gusts. Then, the full picture emerged.

Everything about the boat was white.

The figurehead attached under the protruding bowsprit was easily recognizable, especially adorned with a thorny crown.

A substantive individual, also entirely clad in white, waved a stately wave to the crowd.

"It's the Pope," Alona observed.

"My God," someone gasped.

The Pope gave the slightest of bows.

The ice bridge that formed each Winter between the two Diomedes had disappeared from view. But not far below the ocean surface, its last vestiges 'til the ensuing Fall remained present.

The boat's keel struck it. Hard enough that its primary passenger pitched over the side gunwales, plunging the twenty feet or so into the ice cold sea.

Before the crowd could react, Micmac was flat out heading across the dock. Alongside, Alona with a death grip on his shirt sleeve.

Into an idling, inflatable raft they jumped.

It jarred the craft to the extent the owner pitched overboard.

Alona seized the controls.

Micmac tossed the line.

They headed at flank speed toward the now immobile Holy craft.

They didn't notice, but the entire crowd had broken into a run. Toward the fallen cleric.

"There he is!" Alona yelled. She reduced speed as they floated near.

The Pope, for his part, splashed both arms and yelled out, "I can't swim!"

Alona cut the power.

They drifted close.

The Holy man grasped at the inflatable's sides to no avail.

Micmac fell to his knees. He leaned over the side, and latched onto the nearest flailing arm.

Pull as he might, the former SEAL was unable to do more than keep the Pope's head above water.

"I thought you Christian types could walk on this shit," he muttered.

Alona tried to help.

But Micmac's fingers, icy cold and weakened, lost grip.

The two of them fell backwards.

The top Roman Catholic cleric plunged. His only physical presence represented by two white-sleeved arms flailing at the sky.

Back on the dock, two men arrived ahead of the crowd, and jumped into the raft.

Each latched onto an arm. And pulled with all of their might.

It worked.

The Chief Rabbi and the Grand Ayatollah dragged the Pope up and out over the craft's side.

Now, others pulled on the two men's shirttails.

The concerted effort dumped the soggy cleric onto the boat's flooring.

Realizing he was saved, he glanced up.

His jaw dropped.

"Rabbi Kushner! Grand Ayatollah Jahni! Thank you! And praise the Lord!"

The two produced immediate smiles.

Jahni spoke.

"Now, you owe us."

Kushner nodded. "For saving your sorry ass!"

The Pope shook his head. "What is owed, as Mister Crayle has frequently admonished, is peace. To the world. Everlasting."

The crowd, just a few feet away, heard the entire repartee.

They applauded. They hooted. They hollered.

Before the trio of holy men could react, they heard the engine fire up.

Looking over their shoulders, they spotted Crayle at the helm.

“Back to the fortress, my friends. We’ll get the man,” he referenced the Pope, “into some dry clothes and in front of a warm fire.”

“Let’s all go celebrate the wonderful good deed accomplished by the two spiritual leaders,” he added.

“What about us?” The question emanated from a shivering Micmac as he and Alona clutched together for warmth. “We loosened the lid.”

• • •

The trio of clerics and their impromptu entourage reached the fortress in just fifteen minutes. An hour later they were clad in dry clothes and fed the local fare, sea food. One broke the silence.

“I’ve an announcement,” said the Pope. “It gives me the greatest pleasure to bring …” He looked down at the body he’d brought along. “.. Pattie Norbrunn to sainthood.”

Crayle rushed to the cleric’s side, and whispered in his ear.

The Pope’s jaw dropped. Pattie was the unintended daughter of an Amsterdam prostitute, enabled by the Prince of Monaco. First, CIA rogue agent, then psychopath, then serial killer, and so on.

Then, Hekka got the other ear.

The Pope got the message and responded.

“It was her twin, Nattie, who gave her own life setting up the transformation of Iran back to Persia, who enabled the irreversible march to World Peace. Not Pattie. Nattie. I mean Natalya or Natalie. Yes. Saint Natalie.”

CHAPTER 46

Karl, number one to the leader Otto of the Aryan Alliance, spoke to his boss.

"We only have one bomb. But, as you say, Führer, we must conquer all worthy nations, and obliterate those unworthy. America has to top our conquest list. We do so in a manner that captures their nuclear stockpile. Poof. We have our bombs."

Otto thought. "*Ausgezeichnet!*" he exclaimed. "Outstanding! Except those bombs, unlike our Chinese variant, are huge. And extremely dirty. And non-directional. Unlike our bomb currently undergoing reverse engineering. It is better to eradicate them once we have taken America, and not save them for a rainy day."

"I want to use it. The Chinese bomb. Is it ready?"

"It is not here in Bavaria. It is under study underground at Heidelberg. You know. Our epicenter of German wisdom and genius."

"But what of security? Or earthquakes? It is our only one, and our head of intelligence informed me there are no more."

"One. You question my judgment. Two. You know this intel, as the Americans say, and neglected to inform me?"

Methodically, he reached inside his desk drawer, and removed the black pistol. Its provenance proved it to be the very first Luger pistol created in 1898.

The horrified, transfixed Karl watched as Otto pulled the trigger.

"*Boom!*"

But there was no blood. There was no bullet.

Karl sighed relief out loud.

"I'm shooting blanks these days, my friend. Don't make it hard for me."

"Hard being the medically elusive condition."

On cue, the lovely Maria entered the office. "I heard—"

She stopped when she observed the weapon.

"Oh," said Otto. "It accidentally discharged. While I was threatening Karl."

He turned to his persistent number one.

"You can go now, Karl. My nurse has arrived. She'll make me better."

• • •

Later, Karl gingerly and with trepidation, re-entered Otto's office.

The Aryan Alliance führer looked up.

"If we just have this one miniature nuclear device, Karl, now do we deploy it to our goal?"

"As you would surmise, I've thought deeply about this. The French. They attacked us mercilessly by Napoleon, the Franco-Prussian War, World War I, World War II. They deserve it."

"In your examples, the Prussians won. The world wars … not so."

"But the lesser Europeans needed the Americans as their back stop. Or we would have won."

"Then the answer is simple. Attack America."

"Let's stay on point. The French have reverted back to a monarchy. King Louis XX. We blow up Paris."

"The Illuminé tried that. Mini-nuke devices on the Eiffel Tower. Not as easy as it would seem."

"And what do we gain?"

"Not having that awful tower to point itself at our sky, like an extended middle finger."

"The feeling would be good. But not advance our politic."

"*Es stimmt.* That is correct."

"The Russians?"

"The Czarina Anastasia blew up Moscow. We could undo St. Petersburg. Take out her and her government."

"Great for revenge. But, as with bombing the French, we gain nothing of substance."

Karl pointed his Smartphone at the far wall, and clicked. Up popped a satellite's view of the United States Capitol Mall.

"We must place the bomb and point it such that the force is directed at the Capitol Building, the White House, and the Supreme Court. At a time the president, justices, and congress are present, respectively. There can be no warning. Otherwise, the representatives and senators will scatter like rats. And the president will descend to his bombproof cave."

"What about some other venue? Like Cleveland."

"And risk blowing up the stadium? Or Indians?"

"They are not Indians anymore."

"Oh."

"Washington, D.C., at least a substantial portion of it, has to go."

"When our reverse engineering of the bomb is complete, we shall use the prototype against the Americans. Keep this quiet. President Stones possesses a world-class spy network. On the books or off the books."

"Yes, *Herr Führer*. It was the latter who … who took down your adoptive mother."

"*Jawohl. Meine liebe Mutter*. Yes, indeed. My dear mother."

"We can get that team in Washington at the same time. Avenge Frau Kaari's murder."

"Frau Doktor Mengele, Karl. Like her ancestor Nazi father, a genius of medical research."

He waited a beat.

"Formulate a plan, and a timeline. And the resources we'll need."

"If the bombs are too big, we can cut them apart into smaller, easily concealed and transported weapons."

"These are not veal cutlets to be carved from a trophy deer."

CHAPTER 47

Following the Pope's speech, Crayle and Hekka stepped outside the fortress and walked along a path toward the ocean. Surprising both of them from the other direction, the Northeast, came a couple of people.

From the Island Princess spa.

Crayle performed the introductions.

"Hekka, let me introduce Kelly … and Tracy. They worked the spa services on the ship Micmac and I sailed during my relaxation period."

"Spa? Is that where they give, you know, massages?"

"Strictly on the up and up."

Hekka observed the two pretty ladies, and threw a glance his way.

"Oops?"

A brow wrinkle later, her husband responded.

"Not *that* up and up. Legit up and up."

Kelly could no longer hold the secret.

"He left out the part that we're spies. For The Company?"

Hekka reached out. "How about hugs for The Company teammates?"

Hugs all around.

• • •

They weren't done.

At that point, characters from the Crayle chronicles—the nine novels he'd ripped from the Classified Far Above Top Secret, off-the-books, CIA realities with the factual manifestations of real human beings—began to arrive as if from an orchestrated parade.

• • •

Then, every one of the excursion guides from their journeys showed up.

Crayle lost count.

He thought those he didn't recognize were just due to challenges with his memories.

In fact, there was no way he could know those spy guides from Lenny's recent trip. Or from Hekka's.

• • •

Next came their liaison with French Intelligence. Charleroi still looked to the world like a physical manifestation of the Agatha Christie detective, Hercule Poirot. The thick, curled-up-at-the-ends moustache provided the finishing touch. His agency, *Direction Générale de Securité Extérieure*, would never be the same or as good if he ever retired.

The Frenchman stepped close.

"*Bonjour, Monsieur Crayle.*"

"*Bonjour, Charleroi.*"

Crayle and Charleroi shared a French hug, then backed off a step.

CHAPTER 48

Getting to Eastern Siberia from Germany with a bomb was no easy task. Fortunately, Kamchatka Peninsula still held an enclave evolved from one of Joseph Stalin's prison gulags. He'd created the *convict economy*, the Communist substitute for Capitalism, which they considered pure evil.

At their destination, the Aryan force went below ground. But not in standard fashion. They'd entered a substantial stall marked W.C., for water closet. In this case, the European equivalent to a porta-potty.

Upon depositing individual samples of curly hairs, they were ID'd, and the inside module descended at break neck speed to what, by now, seemed the international requisite depth of 300 feet in seconds. Such ingress was standard for spies and such.

They'd heard the observation deck elevator in Dubai's Burj Khalifa, the world's tallest building, was slightly faster. So, not bad.

There, right outside the elevator doors, sat the rail car.

They fastened tightly the safety harnesses inside the fighter-jet-like canopy. The member with the special rugby ball reversed his backpack to his chest. He wondered how radiation-free was the miniaturized nuclear device inside. He hadn't had kids yet but, being an ideological zealot, he willingly made the sacrifice.

Sitting behind in the fore and aft seating arrangement, his *Führer* could see him shake as paranoia took him in its grasp.

What if 300 miles per hour pulled contacts in the bomb together? What if it detonated? Tight against his chest, it mattered not that it was only five megatons of explosive power.

He glanced inside the backpack. He read the instructions taped over the device in German.

He twisted the fake rugby ball so the **This Side Toward Enemy** faced away.

There.

• • •

The acceleration was smooth. Since the German-engineered tunnel created a vacuum, there was almost no resistance to the high speed.

They covered the distance to their destination in just under ten hours.

Then, out of the cockpit and onto the landing, the German zealot reversed the backpack, and strode off two steps behind his *Führer*.

Through a fresh set of elevator doors, and up.

The leader looked him over, saying, "You don't need to sweat." He waited a beat, then, "Not yet."

The Aryan Alliance would always be, after all.

They knew that the initial Aryan absolutist, Adolf Hitler, absolutely hated Communists. The Aryans had locked themselves into an unholy alliance.

Both leaders climbed into the final balloon.

CHAPTER 49

All had collected for the grand finale.

The first to note were the world leaders.

American President Kimbel Stones, Czarina Anastasia Romanova of Russia and her confidant Raspi, King Louis XX of France, and President Rustom Modi of the new Persia.The only notable absence was Empress Ling of China.

Then, there were the religion contingent.

The Pope, Chief Rabbi Kushner, and the Supreme Ayatollah.

Finally, the Strategic Solutions Office black ops team.

Magus Crayle, Hekka Crayle, Micmac MacKay, Phoebe MacKay, and Alona Lipschitz, with the notable exception of Lenny Lipschitz, still presumed to be somewhere in Canada.

Of all the intensive crew assembled, it was the least likely, Alona, who came up with the grand idea.

"We'll build a bridge from the Chukchi Peninsula to our West and from the Seward Peninsula to our East. To the Diomedes."

"The Bering Sea is too rough," Crayle interceded.

"A bridge over troubled waters," the Pope concluded.

Alona gave him a slap on the back. "Works for me!"

A moment later, channeling her husband, Lenny, "Then, Diomede Disney!"

• • •

Micmac and Crayle were having a good time. They and all the others had been manipulated into showing up on Big Diomede. Each had their suspicions as to the source of the diabolical plot, but were not going to let it spoil the mood.

"Hey, Mag. Let's step over there inside the fort. I want to show you my gadget."

"Save it for Phoebe."

"Not *that* gadget, my new one. For the Science and Technology folks at The Company."

"Okay. But let's make it quick. I don't want to miss anything. It's been quite a happening already. I don't know what could come to upstage what we've seen and heard."

They walked the hundred yards to the fortress, then stepped inside.

They'd just found a quiet and private place when it happened.

"Did you feel that?"

Crayle placed his hand on the floor.

"Maybe they have earthquakes here. Like those we got used to in Southern California."

"This steady. Persistent. Like a deep hum."

"It might be risky, but let's get down into the bowels of this joint, and check things out."

They found their way into the basement, which extended beneath the fortress central open space.

Up ahead, they heard a noise.

As they moved closer in stealth mode, voices.

"German," Crayle whispered. "And Russian. And English."

They arrived at a vantage point where they could see six men, but they themselves remained out of sight.

The men pushed a large, deflated fabric structure tied to a woven basket large enough to contain all six.

Then, beneath the basket they revealed a rugby ball-shaped item attached by cables to the basket.

Two of the men freed it.

Their leader spoke.

Micmac needed a translation.

As quietly as possible, Crayle provided one.

"I recognize him. It's Otto, the leader of the Aryan Alliance. They plan on using the balloon themselves, leaving the mini-nuke behind."

"That bomb will kill us all. Hope for world peace and all would go up in smoke."

"Turn into a fine paste, actually."

At that point, Otto's diatribe was interrupted by his Smartphone chime.

He responded with a few words, then spoke to the others.

"He says we must go lie low for a bit. To allow for any more arrivals. The Russian responded with, "Da. More peaceniks."

The six men left.

• • •

When it was safe, Crayle and Micmac went to work.

The pair departed the scene without a trace.

CHAPTER 50

Later, from the center of the old Russian fortress Big Diomede Island, the lighter-than-air craft and its human contents rose gently. Bolstered by a brisk wind off the Siberian Coast to their West, they headed East.

Completely out of ammo or unarmed, the crowd of the world's religious and political leaders, and the rest below watched the Aryans and exiled Communists escape.

In the balloon's basket, the pilot noticed a shifting back and forth of the weight distribution. The rest of the passengers were not moving. They were heavily engaged in flipping off the extensive Crayle entourage below. It was a behavior they'd borrowed from the Americans—picked up by their own culture during a world war.

The pilot scrambled over the side, hanging on for dear life.

There!

He spotted the mini-nuke Crayle and Micmac had reattached dangling from the basket bottom. It was the swaying effect that produced the weight shifting.

He yanked out his mahogany-handled Hitler Youth dagger, and went after the bomb's tethers.

Far below, Crayle's systems mind assessed the situation in just seconds.

"He'll cut it loose! If he does, we're doomed!"

Next to him, Hekka grabbed her ancient bow. Reluctantly, she fetched the sole arrow from the past. Proof of her indigenous ancestors.

She drew the bow string, allowed for everything, and let the arrow fly.

The projectile flew up and over.

Pushed by the breeze.

Pulled by the gravity.

Foomp!

Just to the right of the Aryan's spine.

There, in severe pain, the man groped with his left hand, grasping for dear life to the basket with his left. It was too much.

He fell, yelling out the entire way.

The others, oblivious and looking over the basket's other side, continued their taunts, unaware that they'd lost their pilot.

Seconds later, they didn't hear the minor league splash into the Bering Sea.

The balloon now headed over the neighboring Little Diomede Island for parts East. On the prevailing winds.

• • •

They all observed as the balloon, bearing the last of the Aryan and Communist hierarchy, drifted East over Little Diomede into American air space. Its trajectory should take it North of Alaska's Seward Peninsula. Toward the pole.

Crayle observed it all on his special phone. With DCI upgrades.

Then, a sound. A loud sound.

Coming from the right.

Necks craned and eyes squinted. No smog to mitigate the brightness of the sun.

Two jet fighters from the Alaskan mainland.

F-22s.

"Crap!" Crayle yelled. "They're hypersensitive about balloons around here! From the Chinese one! From before!"

"It's political," Stones intoned.

"They hit it and the mini-nuke goes off!"

Hekka joined. "Call 'em off, Kimbel! Your special phone!"

The president grabbed from his inside coat pocket. Left side. It was a black phone. The battery icon flashed red.

"Damn!"

Crayle extracted his own device. His CIA Universal Remote, or CUR.

Stones dropped his phone and went for his other inside coat pocket. Right side.

There!

The STU99. He'd wondered what version would come next. Two digits for the sat phone model. Y2K all over again.

The lead F-22 Raptor fired its left-wing missile.

It sped toward the target, a vapor trail in its wake.

Crayle pressed the setup sequence, then pressed PLAY.

The missile was locked on.

500 yards to pay dirt. And nuclear history.

The president verily yelled into the STU.

"This is STONES. Voice encryption ON. Stop the scramble over the Bering Sea! Now!"

Next to him, Crayle pressed PLAY.

The missile detonated fifty yards shy of its target.

The jets veered right. Heading home.

The collective sigh of relief from that many people could've been heard on the neighboring island. On Little Diomede.

"Nicely done, Mag."

The president reached out his hand.

Crayle took it.

"You know it almost didn't work."

"How's that?"

"My self-destruct comms to the missile crossed the International Date Line. I had to get it there yesterday."

"I knew that," Stones piped up.

"Did not," the others chorused.

The sun had passed its apex and headed closer towards China.

Hekka, Alona, Susanna, Luisa, Flori, Marli and others rubbing their arms indicated the chill at this time of day at this latitude even as Spring was springing.

The remaining Aryans and Communists knew they'd dodged a bullet when the incoming missile self-destructed, but still had no idea their mini-nuke dangled just below the balloon's basket. As they were now blown by trade winds in a Northeasterly direction, the cold felt by those on Big Diomede rapidly exceeded that on Yesterday Island, Little Diomede. With no means of control, they'd be over the North Pole soon. With cell service at zero and satellites out of range, they'd have to share body heat until a change in winds blew them South again. To warmer climes.

• • •

Just then, a soggy Micmac, who'd managed to disappear into the Bering Sea briefly, showed up with the Aryan pilot's body slung over his shoulder.

He tossed it on the ground in front of Hekka and, utilizing the Navy SEAL cutlery sheathed to his calf, pried the indigenous arrow free.

Hekka nearly impaled herself as she gave Micmac a big, engaging hug.

Then, Crayle pressed the PLAY button once more.

The crowd watched in awe.

CHAPTER 51

At that moment, Lenny and Darryl, canoeing up their river passage under the brilliance of the neon green Northern Lights above, were surprised to see a balloon tracking in from the West. They did not know that Crayle had pressed the fatal PLAY button.

A gargantuan white-yellow flash.

It set the sky ablaze with intense, vibrant colors.

The Aryan balloon disappeared in an instant.

Mesmerized, not a word was spoken.

Their silence morphed to extreme with the detonation.

The full force of a megaton mini-nuke, even directed upward by Crayle and Micmac's careful positioning, produced plenty of side force to slow the canoe and its occupants.

The shock caused both Lenny and Darryl to drop their oars overboard.

The detonation's downward aspect was diminished by the upward directionality of the bomb.

Still, that brought a water wave.

The canoe seemed fired like a bullet across the bend in the river and up a tributary stream on the South side.

The crisis subsided just as quickly as it began. The breathless duo glanced North.

The green neon curtains had shaken as if by giant invisible hands with the brunt of the '*This Side Toward Enemy*' nuclear device.

"That'll make the news," Lenny gasped.

The Northern Lights quickly regained composure, returning to their natural pose in just a few minutes.

"I hope there weren't any people in that balloon," Darryl uttered.

Lenny picked it up.

"If there were, they won't have to worry about the bears."

He and Darryl realized the oars were gone.

"Well, here we are …"

"Up a creek …"

"Without a paddle."

Darryl finished it off.

"You won't believe the name of this creek. Think excrement."

"Schitt's Creek."

• • •

Back on Big Diomede, the crowd gasped collectively.

What had just happened was clear to all.

The leadership of the Aryan Alliance and the Neo-Communists just melted into nothing in a millisecond.

Those most likely to upset the Peace and Love applecart fronted by the Three Wise Men were gone.

The final Made In China mini-nuke was gone.

Peace had a real chance.

• • •

The three clerics stepped together to take a bow.

The crowd cheered.

Just not at them.

Out on the ocean, another miracle being pointed out by the ever-observant spa ladies.

Another canoe.

Coming their way.

It pulled outboard of Hekka's canoe, and tied up by those on the dock.

As the two occupants struggled to get onto dry land, Alona broke into a run.

She grabbed Lenny, nearly tossing them into the cold Bering Straight.

"Where have you been? You are habitually late … but … that's okay. We can head to the fort. The barracks there have lots of beds, I'm told."

"Alona, my dear. Darryl and I just paddled up the Yukon, then the Mackenzie rivers, across the Arctic top of Alaska, and down the Bering Straight to this place. Destination based on seven little treasure chests."

He shrugged.

"Treasure chests? What for?"

"We used a new S & T app to Un-Scrabble the tiles inside. You know. Tiles? Like in the game? Scrabble?"

"I remember the game. We played it when I was young."

"Long story short, it said PROCEED DIOMEDE. So, here we are."

Crayle, now just a few feet away, added his own intel.

"Same for us, Lenny. We'd stop somewhere on our relaxation cruise." He threw a glare at President Stones. "Picked up the boxes, and did the same with them. Un-Scrabbled the same two words."

Meanwhile, Hekka walked over to the boat deck. She examined the pair of canoes. Cursory, at first. Then, in depth.

"Well, I'll be. They're the same. Same construction. Same details. Hey, everyone. I just won the jackpot. One canoe from Chukchi Eastern Siberia, and one canoe from the Yukon Territory. Proves the link."

"You should check for DNA," Lenny quipped. "You know, of your ancestors."

"It's difficult for me to ignore what you just said," Hekka responded.

"Here. Let me help," Phoebe responded.

It was time for the adult. Time for Crayle.

"Alright, kids. With this find, Hekka can tidy up her PhD research, and receive her crown. Maybe we can get Kimbel to transport these boats down to Big Bear Lake. The locals and tourists will love having them there. Maybe a museum. An indigenous museum. Right at the water's edge."

He wrapped his arms around her in a serious hug.

Just then, Darryl stepped over.

"Hey there, Mag. How the hell are you?"

Maintaining his left arm grip on Hekka, Crayle reached out the other to grasp Darryl's outstretched hand.

"I'm doing fine, Darryl."

He glanced into her eyes.

"Just fine."

• • •

The low frequency thwop-thwop-thwop coming from the West seized everyone's attention. A lone U.S. Marine Corps Osprey VTOL swooped their way. All hands reached for their personal firearms. The landscape was too rough for a landing. As the aircraft neared, the wings rotated into its hovering evolution.

Three ropes tumbled from the aircraft. In seconds, three men descended the thirty foot span.

The first, a slightly portly one dressed in white appeared.

"We just hopped over for a quick visit to Nome," the Pope said. "Alaska? None of us had ever been. This was our big chance. Alaska is definitely proof of God."

They onlookers recognized the Pope's two sidekicks, the Grand Ayatollah and Rabbi Kushner.

"Yes," the Pope continued. "The Three Wise Men. Or so they say."

The other two stepped to a triangular table with the Pope. He supplied a document to which they applied their signatures.

"There," the pontiff declared. "*Pax Orbis.*" He turned to the Muslim. "Do you wish to check my Latin?"

"We Muslims expelled those who spoke Latin."

As the artist he'd been before the clergy, he crafted his own translation into Arabic from right to left just below the *Pax Orbis.*

Lastly, Rabbi Kushner delivered the equivalent Hebrew rendition.

"World Peace," he declared. "Signed into reality."

"Then we shall make it so," replied the Grand Ayatollah in a passable impression of Star Trek's Captain Kirk.

The delta between whim and reality would descend on them over the coming decades, but right now, they didn't care. It was a time of celebration.

"Bring on the bacon!"

• • •

A breeze picked up from the Southwest. There was movement out on the bay. What approached at full sail was an elaboration of a Chinese junk.

As the boat neared, its sailors reefed the sails, sliding it neatly up to the 150-foot pier, and tied it up. Shortly, an entourage debarked and approached.

"Ling!" exuded from multiple sources.

• • •

At this point, they'd all arrived on Diomede. Anastasia, leader of all Russia owned the island. Raspi, too, with a large, multi-page document for Crayle, Hekka, Alona, Lenny, Micmac, Phoebe, President Modi of the new Persia, Jean-Marc, the Swedish queen, and U.S. President Stones, who'd shown up right on cue.

It was no coincidence that Raspi's document was inscribed with a phrase in all languages. At the top, in museum quality script, the words, WORLD PEACE.

CHAPTER 52

It was some time later. Everyone bade farewell, and headed home from Big Diomede. Except Lenny and Alona. They headed East.

Of course, Lenny never shied away from messing up royally.

He'd placed a hood on Alona's head and told her he'd only used it previously during his private investigator work. With burglars, robbers … and just one murderer.

"Surely you washed it in hot water?"

"Uh …"

He paused. Then, "Uh … we're here!"

He helped her from the car and, with great drama, removed the hood.

"Annapolis Valley, Alona!"

She glanced around.

"We're in Maryland?"

"Uh … Nova Scotia."

She took in the storybook scenery—green everywhere—in all directions.

"Turn around."

She did.

"Oh, my!"

He led her into the 1900's period residence.

It was beautiful outside with a spacious, professionally executed interior.

"Oh, Lenny. A body could relax here. And you picked it out?"

"I had a little help."

A tall man stepped out of the bathroom, wiping his hands on his cargo shorts.

"Alona, this is Darryl." He turned. "Darryl … Alona."

The tall, lanky man took her proffered hand.

"Alona, how the hell are you?"

"I am, I think, fine. So you're the travel agent. Nice to meet you. And thanks for all those E-ticket trips you arranged for Team Crayle. And the exfiltrations when things got hot."

"No problem at all, Alona."

"I'm guessing you helped Lenny locate this place. Are you a realtor in your spare time?"

"Oh, no. I just hooked him up with someone who rents the place out. No need for a realtor."

They both turned to Lenny. He bore his signature smirk.

"Actually, I bought the place. Made the owner an offer he couldn't refuse."

Darryl's look passed pale in search of alabaster.

"You didn't …"

"Enough money he could move to San Diego."

Darryl caught the slight. San Diego over Nova Scotia.

"Well, I hope you'll both enjoy it here. I need to leave now. Have to arrange some travel. Off-the-books travel."

"Nice to meet you, Darryl."

"Yeah," Lenny nodded.

• • •

Back in his car and headed northeast toward his home in Sydney, Darryl had a thought.

Living up there in Cape Breton was fine. But, if Lenny would spend any significant time at his new place, he might come up and visit.

Hmmm.

Darryl needed an out.

He had some serious money squirreled away. He'd get his own escape. A personal safe house. Safe from Lenny.

He expressed his conclusion out loud.

"San Diego, here I come!"

CHAPTER 53

A light Spring rain finished its duties over night. The dawn brought the onset of a perfect day. At least, to Southern California's Big Bear Valley.

When Mick MacKay, known to friends and colleagues as Micmac, stepped out on his log cabin's front deck, he had to shield his eyes from the morning sun's glare.

As if by design, his gaze East caught it at just above the mountains with its full force glancing off the lake and into his eyes.

He turned.

"Let's do breakfast out here, my darling Phoebe. Two eggs over hard—as you like things—hash browns, the whole shmear."

He took a seat at the redwood picnic table.

His FBI wife stepped out onto the deck fifteen minutes later. She carried two plates. Their son toddled behind.

"Belgian waffles covered in the superb maple syrup Alona and Lenny sent us from Eastern Canada, whipped cream, bacon, sausage, and sparkling cider to drink."

She sat the plates on the table, and took a seat.

"Just what I wanted," he lied.

She smiled.

"The harsh interrogation techniques will have to wait 'til after breakfast."

His eyes widened.

"Oooh!"

"And if you get it right this time, we'll be setting up that spare bedroom soon."

Micmac peered out at the placid lake.

"Sailors love the water. I'm thinking about putting on my trunks, and getting wet."

"I was thinking along those lines myself. You know. Getting wet."

"What you are thinking about is fabricating a sister for our son. Hmmm?"

"Fabricating? Is that the new 'F' word? So, what am I supposed to say?"

"Let's go fabricate!"

And they did.

And they did get it right.

Blue—on the pregnancy strip.

CHAPTER 54

Over at the Crayle cabin a couple of miles away, Magus, Hekka, and little Kianna had all slept in. Kianna was up around 10 A.M., playing with toys.

Inside the master bedroom, her parents were doing likewise. Only with adult toys.

Finally at 11, the two stepped out into the living room, each hugged their daughter, and then they headed outside to the beautiful day.

"No clouds … and it's lunch time. Serrano burgers on the back deck. Just the three of us."

"Oh. I forgot to tell you. Got an e-message from Alona. They're in their new place—their additional place—in Annapolis Valley. You know, Nova Scotia. She says they love it. They are taking it easy on all the fabulous vineyards and taking little Lenny around to see all the wonderful sights. Even up to Cape Breton and its precious Lac D'Or. And they paid a visit to Darryl in Sydney."

"What's amazing, Hekka, is that you three women on our spy team apparently conceived at exactly the same time."

"How do you know it was?"

"I'm America's intel chief. Remember?"

"But how would you know the exact time of conception?"

"Ah. Hate to say it. Need to know."

He grinned.

"Oh. Do I not have enough clearance?"

He reached for her hand.

"C'mon. Let's go back in the bedroom. We'll see if you have enough clearance."

It turned out she did.

And a little brother for Kianna would soon be on his way.

EPILOGUE

THE RUSSIANS

On Big Diomede Island, Czarina Anastasia said her goodbyes to the Crayle team, and found a spare bedroom in the old fortress. A couple of days later when they headed back to Russia, her trusted main man, Raspi, looked a little worn out.

She'd come to a conclusion. You can have a great relationship with people without having to sleep with them. Who would have thought?

What she did have was a threat-reduced Russian politic with the final Communist remnants evaporated over the Arctic Ocean. She developed a great relationship with Europe and, farther afield, with the United States.

THE FRENCH

Jean-Marc, France's new king, and the Swedish queen engaged in the revelry on Big Diomede Island. Unlike all those attending the ultimate declaration of Peace for the World, he realized he hadn't gotten out much since his coronation.

Gregarious by nature, he enjoyed the vast variety of personages present. Once back in their Parisian palace, the two went to work at generating a centuries-lasting set of heirs to the throne.

THE GERMANS

The final vestige of the extremist Aryan Alliance had disappeared over the Bering Sea. With peace breaking out, the German leadership quickly led the world in seriously reducing their defense posture, and returning the savings to its people. The new chancellor would be cleaning up the country and returning citizens to the venerable Germanic notion of order to all. She instituted a stipend for immigrants who really wanted to return to their mother country. With their mother language. And their mother culture. With worldwide peace had come a worldwide prosperity. From that evolved a new truth—you *could* go home again.

THE SWEDES

The Swedish queen couldn't be happier. Her marriage to the new French king, Jean-Marc, was rock solid. They would work to bring their two seriously dissimilar countries to a common, harmonious unity.

THE PERSIANS

The no longer Iran Middle East mainstay found in its new leader, Rustom Modi, a leader for all. Somehow, he'd come to an agreement with Grand Ayatollah Jahni. There would be a new freedom for all. While everyone was encouraged to engage in religious practices, they would decide their own personal behavior. The One God, not the government, would determine their post life-on-Earth existence. Many discarded the head coverings, and let loose in public the beauty in women the One God created in the first place.

THE ISRAELIS

Chief Rabbi Kushner was of the same mind as the Pope. Following through by replacing the notions of War and Hate with those of Peace and Love. He smiled at the linkage between these 'newfound' notions, and those of the 1960's.

THE VATICAN

Back in his lair, the Pope took particular interest in the outcome on Big Diomede. The presumed differences between the world's three major religions were now dissolved. The indisputable fact that the Creator of Everything created all three to provide guidance assumed that no one of them would dominate—or attempt to dominate—ever again. In all meanings of the term, he'd brought home the bacon.

THE UIGHURS

Arzu ran a tight ship in the newly-created republic of Xinjiang. Transforming from China rule to self rule would have its challenges. She was thankful to have allies such as Empress Ling and, through Magus Crayle, the American president. And other neighboring countries were supportive, and presented no threats.

THE UZBEKIS

Aziza had things under control in Uzbekistan. She'd grown very close to Arzu, not far away in the new republic, Xinjiang. And to Empress Ling. Stability for her people into the far future was the order of the day, and would remain so.

THE CHINESE

Ling continued as Empress of China as her son grew to maturity. She'd chosen advisors and actuators, who would maintain peace and freedom for her citizens far into the future. She'd chosen intellectuals with common sense.

Yellow daughter became the trusted advisor and governed the Hong Kong palace with grace. Harmony among its many inhabitants was the consistent order of the day.

Ties between Ling's China and the new Republic of Xinjiang were as solid as her indelibly solid relationship with its leader, Arzu. And Ling ensured there would be no more nuclear warheads, miniature or otherwise.

Her prosperous relationship with the U.S. president persisted due to her enduring brother-sister-like relationship with Director of Central Intelligence, Mag Crayle.

THE CANADIANS

The Canadians of Nova Scotia, Prince Edward Island, Quebec, and their remote territory called the Yukon survived. They survived Lenny.

THE AMERICANS

President Stones would go on to finish his second term as U.S. President, then retire to Las Vegas. He took Susanna and Luisa with him. He'd intended to leave behind as his legacy a strong, growth economy in the four to six percent range, low inflation, gasoline under two dollars per gallon, and peace throughout the world. And he would do just that.

Lenny had missed some relevant intel when selecting Nova Scotia for a second home. When it was cold and snowbound in Big Bear Valley, it was cold and snowbound in Nova Scotia. It proved to be in the colder weather that one word could travel a long way. "Whine!"

Alona and Little Lenny loved their lives and residences. The toddler not only improved his English language skills as time went on, but picked up some French during their stays in Eastern Canada. Alona continued with her practice in defense law, and Lenny returned full-time to private investigating. He was sure that Crayle would miss him.

Magus and Hekka added a residence near Washington, D.C. He went full-time as Director of Central Intelligence, while she assumed the role of CIA to FBI liaison. She was uniquely qualified.

Little Kianna Crayle, just like the other two team children, looked forward to starting school.

THE CRAYLES

Mag Crayle, now fully installed at Langley as the DCI, took on the role full-time, as he'd promised President Kimbel Stones. But what to do in a peaceful world when the Stones presidency came to an end. Turn over the mantle of the world's premier spy agency ... to Jack Sommers. Perhaps, a cruise. Uh. In a peaceful world. Without bullets flying and bombs bursting. He'd make a serious effort to fill out his new family. As he'd always said, no sacrifice is too big.

Hekka turned in her research paper, and completed all requirements for her Doctor of Philosophy degree. The smiles, laughter, and applause from her husband, Mag, and her daughter, Kianna, made her all warm inside.

THE CULMINATION

Though the last few years had the Crayle team going this way, then that way, then back this way numerous times, it seemed the zigzag was the only way to get from Point A to Point Z. The desired endgame. The actual achievement of the idyllic Xanadu.

Taken all together, it was the Zigzag Xanadu.

The End

ABOUT THE AUTHOR

Committed to international affairs, political intrigue, and espionage, novelist Dennis Bowen has researched his stories in more than 75 countries. He engenders realism and spice in his thrillers due to his wartime service, and his defense and intelligence community background, which led one reader to remark, "Bowen knows his stuff." *The Zigzag Xanadu* follows *The Water Diamonds*, *The Blackstone Perfection*, *The Crystal Seduction*, *The Redrock Quarantine, The Final Masquerade, The Virtue Transition, The Jasmine Negative, The Gospel Labyrinth, and The Kindred Heritage* as the most recent addition to his International Thriller Series. When not traveling the globe to research his next thriller, he resides on the Southern California coast.

Facebook: http://www.facebook.com/DennisBowenThrillers/
Twitter: http://www.twitter.com/DBowenThrillers/
Website: http://www.dennisbowen.com/

AUTHOR'S NOTE

I hope you enjoyed ***The Zigzag Xanadu***. As noted on the cover, this is Book 10 of the ***International Thriller Series***. It stands in addition to the original nine-book series. This note explains, in brief, the process I followed from beginning to end. I decided to include it because there are interesting insights for both readers and aspiring authors.

• • •

How did the original sequential series of seven novels come to be? Prior to my initial writing effort, I would go for bicycle rides around a lake. It was a self-imposed prescription for exercise, fresh air, and a mental time out. Ideas for a story would just pop into my head without any solicitation whatsoever. I'd return home and write them in a notebook. By 2011, I decided to write a novel. The plot would demonstrate how the geopolitical landscape could be severely modified by evil-intentioned malefactors using miniature nuclear devices. I decided to write all the stories in long hand to keep myself physically connected, versus the technological mental distancing inherent with using a computer. After substantial scribblings, annotations, and cross-outs, the words did find their way into the digital orchestration.

Notes on the characters, locations, and scenes grew and grew. I attended a few writers' conferences, read several books, and decided to put pen to paper. So I did. My original estimate, however, would produce a novel of about 750 pages. Too big. I divided the story into three successive novels to make it more manageable, and to provide the initial product to readers much faster.

After three months of putting pen to paper, I realized through epiphany that I'd really gotten to know the story, the settings, and the characters. In fact, I knew the latter so well, I could just keep a mental eye on them, and they could write the scenes. The good news was they couldn't charge me for their efforts. And better yet, I could take all the credit.

As I wrote the three novels, ideas kept coming. By the time I finished them, I had enough notes for two more. Okay, I said. It was meant to be a five novel series. By the time I completed the fifth story, I had notes for two more. The trend led me to pronounce, on more than one occasion, the famous line from the Peanuts cartoon series: Charlie Brown saying, "Good grief!" Or words to that effect. At that point, I considered giving up bicycle riding.

As I noted before, a quite knowledgeable individual whose judgment I trust, deeply familiar with the stories and characters, intimated after reading Book 7, *The Jasmine Negative*, that there just might be an eighth novel required. That was Book 8, *The Gospel Labyrinth*. Then, Book 9, *The Kindred Heritage*. But the characters still were not finished. With ***The Zigzag Xanadu***, I have extended the nine-book series.

Once more. "Good grief!"

• • •

Some, including myself, find that in re-reading any of the ***International Thriller Series*** novels, a reader can enjoy them just as much, or even enjoy them more. You can still get everything in normal, silent reading mode, but I suggest you return to a favorite chapter in this story, read it out loud, visualize the characters and observe the difference.

I do perform a great deal of international research since that is the forum in which my stories take place. Although I plan to finally take a little time off, the ideas never stop coming. Fortunately, I did start a second series I called ***The Backstory Files*** in which I took a second-tier individual from the first series and provided how the title character, ***STONES***, transitioned from a National Security Agency operative to Vice President of the United States in an intense, brief period of time. I have many more characters for which I can write thriller back stories.

And with that, best wishes to all those who've supported my efforts, to all those in foreign lands that have provided precious local flavor intel, and finally to every reader on the entire planet. You are why we do this. Seriously. Thank you. –*Dennis Bowen*

www.ingramcontent.com/pod-product-compliance
Lightning Source LLC
Chambersburg PA
CBHW020611310726
48979CB00008B/1438/J

* 9 7 9 8 9 9 9 7 6 3 2 0 4 *